"You're exquisite," David murmured

Susan closed her eyes and leaned her head back after another spine-melting kiss.

His warm breath on the tops of her breasts made her sigh, and when his fingers traced lazy circles around her lace-covered nipples, she had to steady herself.

David's mouth closed over her right nipple, and even through the material she felt his delicate lips, his teasing tongue. She broke out in goose bumps from head to toe.

His hand slipped around her waist, pulling her tight against him. His erection was no gentle tease this time. It was hard with promise...and intent.

"David," she whispered, opening her eyes.

He mumbled something, not moving an inch.

"Bedroom."

That got his attention. He stood straight, grinned, kissed her hard on the lips, then took her hand. As they passed the ice bucket, he grabbed the champagne bottle by the neck without breaking his stride.

A moment later it was her, him, champagne and a king-size, four-poster bed.

Exquisite, indeed.

Dear Reader,

If you're a Temptation Blaze reader (and who isn't?) you might remember two books from the past couple of years: *Hot and Bothered* and *Ms. Taken*. I've received so many letters asking if my characters, Susan from *Hot and Bothered* and David from *Ms. Taken,* were going to have their own happy endings.

Scent of a Woman is the answer.

This is by far my sexiest book, but it wasn't my fault—honest! I blame it all on Susan and David, who insisted their inhibitions were off limits. Frankly, I was shocked. And intrigued. Well, you'll see what I mean as you read!

Maybe there are some things you can learn from Susan and David. I suggest sneaking away with your significant other to a hotel room, and letting your imagination go wild. Don't forget to wear your sexiest perfume…and nothing else.

I'd love to hear from you. Come visit my Web site at www.joleigh.com. And check out the special Blaze site at www.tryblaze.com.

Happy reading,

Jo Leigh

Books by Jo Leigh

HARLEQUIN BLAZE
2—GOING FOR IT

HARLEQUIN TEMPTATION
756—HOT AND BOTHERED
809—MS. TAKEN

SCENT OF A WOMAN

Jo Leigh

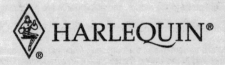

HARLEQUIN®

TORONTO • NEW YORK • LONDON
AMSTERDAM • PARIS • SYDNEY • HAMBURG
STOCKHOLM • ATHENS • TOKYO • MILAN • MADRID
PRAGUE • WARSAW • BUDAPEST • AUCKLAND

This book is dedicated to JJ Medeiros,
for the inspiration, the encouragement
and mostly, for the friendship. Love you.

And to Jack Galle, for helping me to see what's what.

ISBN 0-373-79027-9

SCENT OF A WOMAN

1

SHE KNEW BETTER THAN THIS. Buying new shoes was only a temporary fix. It would lift her spirits for what, an hour? Two? Then she'd be right back in the doldrums.

Susan Carrington shifted her gaze from the display window and forced herself to walk away. She was stronger than shoes, right? Even if they were Jimmy Choos. On sale. And those pink stilettos would be killer with her Dolce & Gabbana duchess satin jacket.

No. She had enough shoes.

The thought made her smile. As if there were ever enough shoes. However, despite the joy they brought, the agony they caused her feet, the jealous looks from complete strangers, shoes could only do so much. They couldn't stop her from wishing things were different. That somewhere out there, and by out there, she meant Manhattan, not the entire planet, there existed her perfect man. Her soul mate. And if she couldn't find her soul mate, then she'd settle for someone hot, hard and gifted.

It had been a long time since she'd been with a man, and her body wasn't thrilled about it. She'd felt restless all week. And not just a little reckless. She wanted...something. Lust, danger, excitement. Shoes simply wouldn't fit the bill. She wanted a man. A nice, juicy, strong guy. Someone with a brain. Someone who knew how to turn her on like a light switch. And wouldn't it be something if her dangerous guy was also her soul mate? Not likely. But she could dream, right?

As she headed down 5th Avenue, she let her imagination go full tilt. She could almost picture him. The unmet stranger. The gaze across a crowded room. He would be tall. At least six-one to go with her five-nine. Dark. Not that blond men were inherently not as cute, but she liked the contrast. A pair of blonds was too Barbie and Ken for her taste.

He'd be handsome, but not pretty. Rugged, but with a smile that changed everything. He'd have expressive eyes, large hands. Large feet. And even though she knew size didn't matter, etcetera, etcetera, he'd have himself an impressive package. Why not? He was her dream man, after all, so she could decorate him however she wanted.

She crossed the street, as always amazed at the pedestrian traffic. It was Monday, the holidays were over, thank God, yet the bustle at one-fifteen in the afternoon was almost as bad as rush hour.

Not that she minded. She loved the rhythm of Manhattan. The pulse of the city. Nowhere on earth was more alive, and even when the curb snow was mostly gray and slushy, and the cabbies laid on their horns as if it would accomplish something, she was at home here.

A bookstore display window slowed her pace to a crawl. She eyed the newest bestsellers, frowning when nothing struck her fancy. Which meant she had to go inside. She tried to remember the last time she'd passed a bookstore and hadn't gone in. No good. She *always* went in.

The music stopped her just inside the door. Wait, wait. She knew it. Closing her eyes, she listened to the symphony, the name of the work teasing her. "Scheherazade," she said aloud, inordinately pleased with herself. She'd always liked the music by... Rimsky-Korsakov. That's right. Ha. Pity one of the gang wasn't with her. She doubted anyone but Peter would have known the piece, let alone the composer.

She opened her eyes again and caught a young man staring. His face reddened and he looked away. Susan brushed the moment aside like so much lint. It had happened before. And before and before. That stare, that slack-jawed ogle. It had, once upon a time, felt wonderful. But after a time, it became clear that the stares weren't about *her* so much as about her parts. Her hair, or her height, or her boobs, or her features. None of which she could take much credit for. She'd gotten lucky in the genetics lottery, but dammit, she wasn't just her looks. At least, she didn't want to be.

She headed down the aisle, wondering if she could bypass the self-help books altogether. She wanted fiction, not transformation. Definitely not soul-searching. Fiction. Make-believe. Stories.

The music swelled, and her thoughts turned to Scheherazade. The woman who'd saved her own life by spinning tales of 1,001 Nights. Ali Baba and the Forty Thieves. Sinbad the Sailor. Aladdin and his magic lamp.

She knew exactly what she'd ask of a genie. Not three wishes, just one. Love. The real thing. The forever kind.

Sadly, it would take a magic lamp to grant her that wish. She and love were on pretty shaky ground. Her one real shot at it had ended abysmally when she'd discovered the man she'd given her heart and soul to hadn't been interested in her at all. Just her parts. And her money. Mostly, her money.

Sighing, she looked at a few books, but gave that up when she couldn't focus. This was bad. Normally, she wasn't such a goose, but dammit, seeing Katy and Lee at breakfast had made her think. They'd bitched about how awful they felt, how they wished the time would come already, how being almost nine months pregnant was anything but a picnic. Susan had laughed and made sympathetic noises, but jealousy swirled inside her, making her food taste like cardboard and her guilt swell with every breath.

She loved Katy and Lee, and their husbands Ben and Trevor. Along with Peter, they were her closest friends in the world. Her family. They'd all met in college, and had never lost touch. The six of them were still thick as thieves, and they'd gone through all the trials and tribulations of work, love and heartbreak together.

But after the other two women had become pregnant, she'd felt distanced. She'd done her best not to show it, but they knew. She was the odd man out, the third wheel. And she hated it.

She wanted a baby growing inside her. She wanted a husband who loved her for *her*. Instead of buying books, she should be shopping for magic lamps. And praying for a genie. Given her luck with men, her penchant for finding money-hungry jerks, magic was about her only hope.

DR. DAVID LEVINSON STARED at the array of shawls and scarves on the shelves in front of him. He should have thought this through before heading into the small boutique. He knew nothing about women's clothing. His secretary had sworn he'd earn major bonus points by giving his sister a scarf for her birthday, but perhaps a few CDs or DVDs would be just as good.

He walked further into the shop, and lifted a silky scarf, unfolding it to reveal the intricate pattern. Too fussy for Karen. He checked the price tag and quickly folded the garment, putting it back. Eight hundred dollars? For a scarf? Jeez. He'd had no idea.

Not that his little sister wasn't worth the money, but man, eight hundred bucks? He went to another display. Pashmina. He'd never even heard of it. The shawls were woven, and looked incredibly soft. On the counter next to them was a similar display of cashmere shawls. There didn't seem to be much of a difference. Only the pashmina shawls were a lot more expensive.

"Close your eyes."

David started at the voice, very close, behind his right shoulder. He began to turn, but a hand on his shoulder stopped him.

"Go on. Close your eyes."

The voice sounded as silky as the cashmere. As sensual as silk. But close his eyes?

"It's all right," she whispered again, this time so close he felt warm breath on the back of his neck.

He obeyed, and the idea that he obeyed without knowing who she was, or what she intended, was as much of a rush as the scent of the woman behind him. He felt her move, and it was all he could do not to peek. She was tall, that much he knew because her breath—

Something brushed his cheek and he jumped, but again, her hand on his shoulder made him still.

"Don't think. Don't analyze. Just let yourself feel," she whispered.

The material caressed the side of his face, delicate, soft, lush, like the skin on the inside of a woman's thigh. Then it was gone, and just as he was about to complain something slightly different brushed his right cheek. Cooler. Slightly thicker. A more earthy scent.

As the cloth slid across his face, he became aware of the effect this exercise was having in a completely different part of his body. He was aroused. Nothing life threatening. Not yet. But between the feel of the cashmere and the mystery of the woman, he was growing more uncomfortable by the second.

The material was withdrawn. He hesitated, waiting to see if there was more.

"You can open your eyes now."

Again, he obeyed. She was directly in front of him, smiling coyly with perfect lips. He'd been correct, she was tall. But his imagination hadn't been up to the task of picturing the rest of her.

Pale blond hair in a graceful tangle, held by a tortoiseshell clip. Wide blue eyes under arched brows. Stunning.

"Which did you like better?"

He blinked.

"The right cheek or the left?"

"Oh."

Her smile broadened, revealing even white teeth.

"The left," he said.

"That's pashmina. The wool is from Nepal, taken from the Himalayan goat. Finer than cashmere. This one," she held up a black shawl, "is an eighty-twenty blend."

"Okay."

Her laughter made his predicament worsen. He shifted a bit, but that didn't help. His slacks were getting tighter by the second.

Her gaze darted to his left hand, then back up to his face. "For your wife?"

"Sister."

"How thoughtful."

"She's a good kid."

The woman nodded slowly, never taking her eyes from his. It was blatantly sexual. There was no misinterpreting her intention. She knew what her gaze was doing to him.

"So, what's it going to be?"

"Pardon?"

She held up the shawl in her left hand. "Pashmina?'' Then she lifted her right hand. ''Or cash-mere?''

''You're good at this,'' he said.

''At what?''

''Your job. I hope you work on commission.''

''I don't work here.''

She'd done it again. Surprised him. Nothing much surprised him these days. Being a psychiatrist in New York tended to jade a person. ''And yet you know about Himalayan goats.''

She laughed again, turning up the heat. Intentionally? Yes. Oh, yes.

''I'm a virtual font of insignificant data,'' she said. ''I am to real knowledge what an onion is to a martini.''

He reached over and took the pashmina shawl from her hand, letting his fingers brush hers. Mistake. The somewhat vague threat in his pants turned dangerous. He couldn't remember the last time this had happened to him. College? Probably. Not that he didn't get excited by certain women. But he rarely reacted in such a volatile fashion. He used the shawl to cover his embarrassment. She might know that she was turning him on. She didn't need to know to what degree.

''I imagine you know quite a bit, Ms....''

She started to answer him, then stopped. She boldly studied him for a long self-conscious moment. Then her smile returned. Only this time there was more than a hint of wickedness in the grin. ''Scheherazade.''

''You're not serious.''

''I am.''

"Your real name is Scheherazade?"

She shrugged, and the movement made him aware of the shawl she had around her shoulders. During the whole conversation, he hadn't even noticed. It was dark gray, and even without touching it, he knew it was pashmina. She'd never settle for second best.

"And who am I supposed to be? Sinbad? Aladdin?"

She took a step toward him, invading his personal space. Which was fine, except that he had some trouble breathing.

"Who do you want to be?"

"Right now I wouldn't want to be anyone on earth but me."

"Excellent answer."

"So what do people call you? Sher?"

"No. But you may."

He was about to comment, but a single finger touched his lips. An incredibly intimate gesture, something a lover would do. Not a stranger using a false name. Not a woman so beautiful it hurt.

She leaned over until her lips were close to his ear, close enough for him to feel her breath once more. "Why don't we talk about this Wednesday night. At the Versailles hotel bar. Eight o'clock."

Then she did the most remarkable thing. She nipped his earlobe. It didn't hurt. It only lasted a second. But it was the single most erotic thing that had ever happened to him. By the time he was cogent enough to exhale, she was gone. He spun around, just in time to see her slip out the boutique door.

What in hell? Was that for real? Was *she?*

Wednesday night he had dinner plans with his friends Charley and Jane. He liked Charley and Jane. His dinners with them were the highlight of his week. He never cancelled.

He rubbed the shawl between his hands.

They'd get over it.

FIVE BLOCKS FROM THE BOUTIQUE, Susan slipped inside a coffee shop and found an empty booth. Her heart rate was in the scary zone, pumping with enough adrenaline to jump-start a dead battery. What the hell had she just done?

Okay, he was very handsome. But handsome men were a dime a dozen in Manhattan. Handsome didn't explain her outrageous behavior. Well, there was that lower lip. Full in just the right way. Exceedingly kissable. And his eyes. Hazel leaning toward green. Bedroom eyes. Knowing eyes. Not to mention long, beautiful hands.

Which was not the point. Not at all. Wasn't she just bitching about the fact that all men saw were her looks? That she was more than her parts? Did she just pick up a strange man because he was *pretty?*

No. That he was gorgeous was a bonus, not the reason. She couldn't pinpoint her real motivation, not in words. It had been more of a feeling. A compulsion. The moment she'd laid eyes on him, she'd felt…something.

The waitress approached on squeaky shoes and took her order for coffee and a plain bagel, no cream cheese, no butter. When Susan was alone again, she got her cell phone from her purse and hit speed dial two.

"Hello?"

"Lee, it's me."

"Hey."

Susan opened her mouth to tell her girlfriend about what she'd done. Only no words came out.

"Susan?"

Why was she hesitating? She told her friends everything. In detail. So what was the problem? This whole thing was nuts.

"Susan, are you all right?"

The concern in Lee's voice snapped her out of her mini fugue state. "Yeah. I'm fine. Just distracted for a minute. How are you feeling?"

"Huge."

"This too shall pass."

Lee sighed. "Yeah? When?"

"In about two months."

"Susan, what's going on? You don't sound like yourself."

"I walked away from a pair of Jimmy Choo mules. I didn't even try them on."

"Ahhh. Now I get it. That was very brave. Very empowering."

"Empowering, my ass. They were the exact color of my duchess jacket."

"If you still feel that way, go back."

"No, no. I can be strong."

"Good girl."

The waitress came and filled her cup with coffee. "My food's here," she said. "I'll call you later."

"'Kay. Bye."

Susan disconnected, then stared at the phone for a few moments. Mighty peculiar. She'd never made an excuse to get off the line with Lee. Or any of her friends. But the man in the camel coat wouldn't let her alone.

Tall, lean, broad-shouldered, brown thick hair her fingers ached to touch. She lifted her cup to take a sip, then nearly spit a mouthful all over the table.

She'd bitten his earlobe!

A perfect stranger. Not a lover. Not even a friend. She'd bitten him. He must have thought she was a lunatic. Or a call girl. Either way, she hadn't come out smelling like a rose.

She'd propositioned him. Teased him. Pretty much offered herself up on a silver platter. Which was ludicrous. She couldn't possibly go to the Versailles Wednesday night. Sure, she talked a good game, daydreamed with the best of them, but the reality was, sex wasn't an easy answer for her. She tended to confuse it with love, and then she tended to trust the son of a bitch, and then she tended to get her heart broken. Her dismal track record was reason enough not to pursue this.

He was a stranger. A good-looking stranger, but a stranger nonetheless. He could be a bank robber. A spy. A car salesman.

She smiled, thinking about the name she'd given him. Scheherazade. It had been the scarves, the music from the bookstore. Just a lark. A whim.

But she had to admit, the idea of being someone else held appeal. Would Larry have pursued her so single-mindedly if he hadn't known she was Susan Carrington, heir to the Carrington fortune? Probably not. Definitely not.

The fact of her inheritance had been the death knell to every relationship she'd had since college. Even when she'd gone out with men wealthy in their own right, the money thing became a problem. It was her personal albatross. She avoided society parties like the plague. In fact, all her friends were just normal folk. Not a multimillionaire in the bunch. But it didn't matter. As soon as a man found out her name, the jig was up. They tried to impress her. Act as if it didn't matter, which meant it mattered a whole lot. They stopped seeing her as their brains clouded over with dollar signs.

At least she'd managed to temper some of her bitterness. Not that she wasn't still cynical. She just didn't want to neuter the male population any more. It wasn't all of them that were bad, just the ones she chose.

The worst part was, she couldn't complain. Not in good conscience. She had it all, the American dream, the brass ring. Except that all it had done was make her feel different, separate. She felt safe with her gang, and that was about the only place she felt safe. Thank goodness for them.

But Ben was married to Katy, Trevor was married to Lee and Peter was gay with a significant other of his own. No hope for a happy-ever-after there. They'd tried setting her up. Over and over, Katy and Ben in particular had played matchmaker. Nothing clicked.

At twenty-seven, she had no prospects. None at all.

She could buy Jimmy Choo shoes until she got blue in the face, and it wasn't going to help. It was all about money. Spending it, having it, worrying about it.

Lee had asked her once why, if the money was such a problem, she didn't give it all away. Susan had uttered some slick answer then changed the subject. The truth was that the money was her blessing and her curse. She didn't know who she'd be without it. Frankly, she was scared to be without it.

Her head snapped up and she pulled herself out of the self-pitying hole she'd dug. Of all the problems to have, hers was right up there in the obnoxious range. She was pretty and loaded. Yeah. Boo hoo. Besides, rich people got married every day of the week. They got married, had kids…just like real people.

She thought of all the happy rich couples she knew… There had to be at least one happy couple, right? Her bagel came, and she ate the entire thing, plus another cup of coffee, and still she couldn't think of one blissful union among her peers. The marriages were more like mergers. And it was almost incestuous, because the people in the inner circle always ended up with other people in the inner circle.

The man in the boutique was an outsider. Which was a very good thing. He had no idea who she was, which was another very good thing.

She smiled. Who says he ever had to know who she was? Why couldn't she be Scheherazade? At least for a night. And maybe, like the woman from the

Arabian Nights, she could spin him a tale, enchant him with the magic of a story.

The bottom line was that she wanted to see him again. She didn't want to know what he did for a living, who his parents were, how terrific his portfolio was. She wanted what she'd had for those few minutes in the shop.

When he'd touched her finger, she'd felt a jolt run through her. A purely sexual rush.

He might not come. In all likelihood, he probably thought she was a wacko.

But then again, he might come.

She bit her lower lip and shifted on the booth. Who knows? They might both come.

2

"WHO'S ON THE BOOKS today, Phyllis?" David asked cheerfully on Tuesday morning. He put his briefcase under his desk, then turned to his secretary. Phyllis had been with him for four years, and she ran his office with great good sense and a necessary sense of humor. And she was the soul of discretion, which was critical with his clientele.

"Mr. Travolta had to postpone for two weeks. He's flying to California. You've got Mr. Broderick at eleven, lunch with your sister at one, and Mr. Warren at three."

"Great. Give me a half hour, and then let's do some dictation, okay?"

"Right. Coffee?"

He nodded. "Thanks."

Phyllis smiled as she walked out of his office, and as soon as she closed the door, he dialed Charley. He had to leave a message, and when he tried Jane, he got the answering machine. Frankly, he was relieved. He had to figure out what to tell them—why he couldn't make dinner tomorrow night. Not that he wanted to lie, exactly. But he could just see Charley's face when he told them he was breaking their long-standing engagement to meet a strange woman at a hotel. And that he didn't even know her name.

Phyllis came back with his coffee, then quietly retreated. The woman was in her fifties, but she appeared much younger. Perhaps it was her red hair, worn loose to her shoulders. Or maybe it was her sense of style. She always looked pulled together, and she was unfailingly serene amid the chaos that went along with having famous patients.

He wasn't sure even now how he'd ended up with so many celebrity clients. It had started about two and a half years ago with a soap opera actress. She'd recommended a highly acclaimed actor friend, and it had mushroomed from there.

He didn't mind. It was fascinating to explore the kinds of problems that went along with fame and fortune. The only real problem for him was the paparazzi. They tended to lurk downstairs and question him as he came and went. They bothered Phyllis, too, but not often. She was an expert at chasing them away.

He sipped his coffee, then turned in his chair. His view from the high-rise was spectacular, and he realized that lately, he'd been so busy he hadn't taken even a few moments to enjoy it.

The park was covered in snow, and it looked like a postcard from Currier & Ives. January was a good month for New York. It made the city appear innocent, which was quite a feat. In March, the magic would be over, when the white gave way to gray, but for now, at this height, it was all magic.

His gaze moved in the direction of the Versailles

hotel. He'd never been there, but he'd read about it. It was one of the new boutique hotels, catering mostly to the European trade. Was he really going to meet her there? A complete stranger? What if she was a reporter, and all this was a trick to get some information on a client?

No, that wasn't possible. No one could have known he'd walk into that store, and she must have been there before he'd arrived.

His hand went to his ear, and he rubbed the lobe where she'd bit him. Talk about leaving a mark. Although there was no sign of her teeth—it had been a gentle nip—the echo of the startling move had stayed with him all night. He closed his eyes, remembering his first impression of the woman.

She was a class act. The shawl wasn't the only sign. Her makeup was subtle, but perfect. Her skin pampered. The diamonds in her earrings looked like the real McCoy. But more than that, the way she carried herself, her confidence, her audacity, bespoke the kind of rearing and education that came with old money. He'd seen it often enough to recognize the signs.

He had a few patients who were the same type, but he had the feeling none of them were in her league. He wasn't, either. Not that he was complaining. His practice had flourished, his portfolio had done very well, and he was one of the fortunate who could actually afford to live in Manhattan. To live well, that is.

He realized he was rubbing his ear again, and he tried to catalogue what else he'd noticed about *Sche-*

herazade. Ridiculous name, but intriguing, too. Of course he knew the story. The princess Scheherazade had been sentenced to death by a wicked king, but she held the king spellbound with her nightly tales, always stopping before the denouement, so he was compelled to let her live another day.

Is that what his mystery woman was going to do with him? Tell him tales? Keep him in suspense? The idea appealed. He liked the element of surprise. He hadn't realized what a rut he'd been in until yesterday at that boutique. Sher had shoved him out of his comfort zone. Quite firmly.

Even though his night had been filled with feverish dreams, he felt more alive today than he had in years. Eight o'clock tomorrow night. He couldn't wait.

SHE WASN'T GOING.

The whole idea was ludicrous.

Besides, he wasn't going to show.

Susan looked at her reflection in the mirror, although she couldn't see too much of herself. Not with the mint-green mud mask on. But her eyes were clear, and that's what she studied. They were the window to the soul, right? So what was her soul trying to tell her? Yes? No?

Dammit. Her eyes weren't talking. She left the bathroom and climbed onto her bed. The one place on earth she was perfectly at peace.

Yes, she knew she had too many pillows. But she didn't care. It was her bed, and she could make it any way she pleased.

Her shoulders sagged with the realization that no

one cared one whit about her pillows. She'd reacted to a long-ago conversation with a man she couldn't stand. Larry had hated the pillows. They'd fought. Over and over. Eventually, she'd given in and tossed the pillows. Her gesture hadn't saved the marriage.

Nothing could have. Not counseling, not acquiescence, not a change in her outlook. The man had wanted to milk her dry. Period. There was no love there. Sadly, there had never been love, at least not from him. Not with Larry or any other man.

She wished she had a Trevor. Lee's idea a year and a half ago to add sex to their friendship had turned out to be the best move Lee had ever made. Their marriage was a wonder to behold. Friends. Lovers. Mates.

She flipped the TV on, shaking herself out of her reverie. It wasn't like her to be so morose. So fatalistic. Sarcastic and cynical? Sure. But mopey? Not her style.

Another click of the remote control and she paused at an old black-and-white Bette Davis movie. *Now, Voyager.* It had been one of her favorite films. She loved the way Bette Davis transformed from the ugly duckling into the beautiful swan. But as she watched the ending, Bette and Paul Henreid talking about their unrequited love, she shook her head. And then, the famous last line:

"Oh, Jerry, don't let's ask for the moon. We have the stars."

"Hogwash," Susan said to the screen. "You deserve the moon." She snuggled against her pillows. "We all deserve the moon."

Screw it. She *would* go. In fact... Her phone was in her hand and she called the hotel. She debated for a moment after the reservation clerk asked if he could help. Then she threw caution to the wind and booked a suite.

Once she hung up, her nerves got busy, illustrating in their own unique way that while her mind had confidently moved forward, heeding the call to adventure, her body was trying like hell to shrink back and stay in the cave. Her life might be dull and ordinary, but it was safe. Too safe.

She was going. Tomorrow night. To a rendezvous with a beautiful stranger. Holy cow.

"WHAT'S WITH SUSAN?"

Lee Templeton dug into her crème brûlée with gusto, even as she bemoaned her current state of hugeness. After savoring her spoonful, she looked up at Katy, who was even larger, given she was eight months along. "What do you mean?"

"Have you talked to her lately? She's being very odd."

"How can you tell?"

Katy giggled. "Odd for her. She's doing something tonight, but she won't say what."

"Huh." Lee put her spoon down and took a big swig of milk. She shuddered a bit, not ever having been a big milk fan. But she'd do anything for her baby. Her hand went protectively to her stomach. "You think it's something about Larry?"

"I don't know." Katy ate a delicate piece of arugula, splashed with a hint of balsamic vinegar.

Lee frowned with disgust. Pregnant women were supposed to have cravings for weird things. Sweet things. Not arugula, for heaven's sake. "It's probably nothing," she said, remembering about Susan.

"Yeah? When's the last time she tried to keep a secret from us?"

Lee didn't have to think long. "That time she was dating that guy. That poet."

Katy's right brow rose.

"You think she's seeing someone?"

"Well…"

"God, remember how awful he was? It wouldn't have been so bad if he hadn't written such terrible poetry."

"Or if he hadn't been so damn proud of his abject poverty."

"Or if he hadn't had a face like a fireplug."

Lee grinned. "We're horrible."

"No. We're gossips. *He* was horrible."

"She got over him quickly enough."

"One date was too many."

Lee went back to her dessert. "So you think she's found another one?"

"Maybe. She did promise to give the love thing another try. Although, I'm not convinced she's completely ready."

"Think we should press her?"

"Not yet," Katy said, after a moment. "It may just be a one-time thing—an experiment or something. If that's the case, there's no need to worry."

"Where Susan is concerned there's always need to worry."

"I know. Especially lately. She's been down."

Lee nodded. "I think she's feeling left out."

Katy's hand went to her tummy. "Yeah."

"So I don't want to, you know."

"Right." Katy took another bite of salad. "We'll let it go. See what happens."

"Keep our ears open."

"And call her first thing tomorrow morning."

Lee nodded. Then the crème brûlée captured her attention until the very last bite.

DAVID WALKED DOWN Club Row, 44th Street, in Midtown Manhattan. He knew the street well, mostly because of the Bar Association headquarters, but also from going to the theater. His breath came out in sharp puffs of condensed air, and when he inhaled, it was cold enough to sting. But it wasn't snowing, and the bitter weather wasn't severe enough to keep most intrepid New Yorkers at home.

He stopped outside The Versailles. The beautiful old hotel with its green and brown awnings. He tried to remember the name of the hotel that was here before. As soon as he stepped into the lobby the question vanished, replaced by the thoughts that had plagued him most of the day.

What was he doing here? Aside from the fact that he hadn't made love in an uncomfortably long time. And that the woman in question was stunning and mysterious and bold. And that she'd asked him.

He walked slowly through the inviting lobby with its teakwood paneling, marble floors, and clusters of oversized velvety furniture. The hotel wasn't big, not near the size of say The Plaza, but it screamed wealth.

It said something about the woman that she'd chosen this place. A certain sophistication. A certain pocketbook. Or not. Oh, for God's sake, who cared? He wasn't here to discuss the architecture or the guests. At least he hoped not.

He stopped and glanced at his watch. One minute early. All he had to do was turn left and walk into the bar. She'd either be waiting for him, or she wouldn't. He wasn't at all sure which outcome he preferred.

After raking a hand through his hair, taking a deep breath, squaring his shoulders—he exhaled, then cursed himself for a fool. What had happened to him? Had be become so old that he couldn't walk into a bar to pursue what might be an extraordinary adventure? In college, he'd been a madman. Yes, he'd studied, but that wasn't the thing. He'd explored. He'd dared. He'd fallen flat on his face.

But it hadn't mattered. He'd wanted all life had to offer back then. What did he want now? Safety? Security? Yes. But that was the white bread of life. He also wanted spice. Heat. Daring. Dammit, he wanted Tabasco sauce, and plenty of it.

He turned left and started walking. What the hell. The worst that could happen was… Hmm. He had no idea what the worst was. But he could clearly imagine the best.

SUSAN LIFTED HER MARTINI to her lips, pleased that her hand barely trembled. Inside, she was a mess.

Scared wasn't the half of it. But on the outside, in the tradition of her mother and her grandmother, she was cool, calm, collected. It was a hard-won skill, but she'd had a lot of practice.

Her mother had told her over and over that emotions had no place on the negotiation table. And what was the whole man/woman thing but negotiation?

This was her party. She'd extended the invitation, prepared the room, including the party favors, and now, it was up to her to make certain everything went according to plan. No problem. Except perhaps for one detail: she had no idea what she was going to do with Mr. Gorgeous once she got him upstairs.

He'd expect her to sleep with him, but was that what she wanted? A brief, sweaty interlude on a cold winter's night?

Maybe.

But something told her that she'd be cheating both of them by jumping right into bed. The man, God, how could she not know his name, had something special about him. Nothing she could pinpoint. Not his looks. Something in his eyes, in the way he smiled. She remembered that smile perfectly—how his teeth were very white, but not perfectly even. The small flaw made him infinitely more appealing, although she wasn't sure why.

The music from the bookstore spun in her head, and with it came an idea. A way to make tonight perfect. Scheherazade. She was the answer. Susan smiled as the evening unfolded in her mind's eye. It would be lovely. If he went along with her.

Another sip of the cold drink as she looked around

the bar. It was very small as far as hotel bars went. But it was comfortable with its dark oak and wine leather booths. This was her turf. Nothing could go wrong here, not in the serious sense. Well, that wasn't quite true. She could be stood up. Humiliated.

She ran a hand down her dress and forced herself to steer clear of those thoughts. She should have worn the black Prada. No. This one was better. Simpler. A wave of nervous tension hit her in the stomach. Oh, jeez, what if she threw up all over him? What if her plan was foolish and awkward?

This was a serious mistake. Sure, she'd felt reckless, restless, but this was taking things too far. She'd leave, and forget she'd ever thought of such a crazy—

"Hello."

Susan jerked up to see Mr. Gorgeous not two feet away. Holy… She had to struggle to keep the expression out of her face. It would blow everything all to hell if he knew that her heart thumped against her chest as if it was trying to get out. "Hello," she said back, thankful for all the years she'd practiced being a bitch. She had the exact right tone. Low, sexy, in charge.

He smiled, held out his hand. "David."

"Su—"

"Sue?"

She nodded. "For now."

"Not Scheherazade?"

She slipped her hand into his, and when he closed his fingers, she felt herself slide another inch down the long treacherous slope of pure insanity. "No. But there are similarities."

David held on to her hand while his left brow arched. "Is the King of Persia bothering you again? Because I've told him time and time again—"

She laughed, but not loudly enough that she missed the slight hitch in his breath. When he swallowed, making his Adam's apple bob, she knew he was just as nervous as she was. My God, he was pretty. Which wasn't the important part, she knew that. It sure as hell didn't hurt, though.

"May I?" he asked, finally taking his hand away and sliding onto the stool next to hers.

The bartender came and took his order, a scotch, neat. She shook her head when David offered to refill her martini. This was no time to hide behind an alcoholic haze. Just being near him was a bit intoxicating, and if she threw in the fact that their suite was waiting...

"Are you all right?"

She nodded. Smiled. "I didn't think you'd be here, either."

He smiled back, making her want to lick his lower lip. "I'm not sure why I did come," he said. "I, uh, don't usually..."

"Go out with women who bite your ear?"

Even in the dim light of the bar, she could see him flush. A man who blushed! What a treat. What a rarity. How delicious.

"I confess, that was a first for me."

"Me, too."

"So nibbling on ears isn't your standard icebreaker?"

She shook her head. "No."

"Hmm. How did I get so lucky?"

Susan took a slow sip of her drink, stalling for time as she made her decision about the next few minutes. She liked him. The chemistry was undeniable, and he had a sense of humor, too. He wasn't at all the kind of man she wanted for a one-night stand. But maybe this didn't have to be. Maybe, if she was a clever girl, this could be a prelude. To what, she wasn't sure. But, despite the risks, or maybe because of them, she was going to find out.

She put her glass down, then turned to him with her most wicked and enticing smile. "If you think that was lucky…"

3

DAVID FINISHED HIS SCOTCH in one gulp and managed not to choke to death.

Her words still shimmered in the air, their meaning sinking in one vivid image at a time. He struggled for focus, finding it when his gaze met her lips. Full, lush lips. That would look incredible wrapped around his—

"Maybe not *that* lucky," she said, her low voice tinged with humor.

He cleared his throat, troubled that his expression had been so unguarded. "Okay," he said, amazed he sounded somewhat normal. "How lucky?"

"You'll see." She caught the bartender's attention, nodded, then slipped off the bar stool. She picked up her purse and coat from beside her, then turned to him. Her lashes lowered, shyly, then she opened her eyes and met his gaze. The invitation in her gaze told him most of what he needed to know.

He stood, then went for his wallet.

"It's taken care of," she said.

"Wait a minute—"

"Don't worry about it. Tonight's on me. I invited you, remember?"

"I don't—"

She put one finger on his lips. "We can talk about money for as long as you like. Or we can go upstairs."

He took her wrist in his hand, then headed for the elevators, pulling her along after him. Forcing himself not to run.

He was in. Committed. To whatever was going to happen.

Charley would be shocked out of his mind. Jane would understand completely.

This wasn't his normal modus operandi. When he dated, which wasn't that often anymore, he always did the right thing. Maybe a kiss on the first date. Flowers. Three, maybe four dates later, if it ever got that far, there would be sex. Safe sex. And not just because he used a condom. It was safe in every way. He never truly let go, too afraid to upset the very nice women he found himself with. Sometimes, they'd get a little wild, like sex in the shower, or on the kitchen table.

But the sex, even when it was very good, had never been enough. Not that the women he'd met weren't great. They were to a one. But none of them had been *right*. One was too flighty, one too prissy. Kathy had been close, but the woman hadn't read a book since high school. Allison never shut up. Kim, no, Kerry, she'd been fine in the bedroom but awful in public. Her laugh had been loud, garish...

Tonight, none of that mattered. Tonight, he wasn't Dr. David Levinson. He was a stranger. Meeting a stranger. Who could be anyone.

The ideas tumbled inside him, one more enticing

than the next. He was already hard, and they were still in the lobby. He'd have to slow himself down if he wanted tonight to be everything it promised. He said a silent prayer to whoever was listening. *Please*.

Susan clutched her coat, each step making her more and more aware of what she was about to do. In very short order she was going to be in a room, which was primarily a bed, with a man she hardly knew. A man whose touch made all sorts of unpredictable things happen inside her.

They were across the lobby in no time, then he pushed the button for the elevator. He hadn't let her go, and she became terribly aware of his hand circling her wrist. He was long and lean, a runner or a swimmer she'd guess, and strong. She felt his banked energy in the way he held her so carefully. As if he could break her.

Her gaze met his, and her own curiosity was echoed in his eyes.

"Sue," he said softly, trying her name out.

Unfortunately, she hated being called Sue. It rankled each time she heard it, which wasn't in the game plan for the night. "Susan."

He nodded slowly. "Better."

The elevator arrived, and he led her inside. They were alone, they could have talked, but they didn't. The only thing that happened was that David rubbed the inside of her wrist with his thumb. No biggie. Just a slight caress. But the ripples it set off were very big, indeed. Straight up her arm to her chest to her tummy to her thighs and every place in between. A tightness, an electricity, a chemical reaction that made it difficult to breathe.

The tension broke as the door opened on the fifteenth floor. It was her turn to lead. They went all the way to the end of the hall. He let her go so she could get the card key from her purse. Her fingers shook as she slipped the card in, and she almost laughed. She'd thought the tension in the elevator had been bad.

He pushed open the door and as soon as she walked inside, he followed, closed the door and locked it. Susan's gaze went straight to the bedroom.

It was a beautiful suite, an eclectic mix of oriental and European sensibilities with stunning modern art that somehow made the whole thing work. The space was large, for Manhattan, with a nice sitting room, a wet bar, and, of course, the bedroom. She could see the bed from there. Unique for a hotel because of the wrought iron head and baseboards, it was also a California king, big enough for three. Not that she'd ever know that firsthand. Oh, God. Maybe this was a mistake. A colossal error in judgment. There was still time to back out.

She turned to David, and his excitement fairly vibrated. Which made sense. It was exciting. And dangerous. And wicked as all get-out. Well, if she was going to go down in flames, she wanted to do it with this man. He was extraordinarily beautiful, in a completely masculine way. Granted, his jaw was too square, his nose too big, but that added to his attractiveness. If she'd been a painter, she would have done canvas after canvas of his face, from every angle possible. Something told her it would be time well spent.

He took her coat from her arm. "Would you like me to order drinks?"

She nodded. "Champagne?"

"Good. Anything else?"

"Not unless you're hungry."

His lips curved into a sort of grin.

"What?"

"This is a most unusual night."

She grinned back. "I would have to agree."

"What are your thoughts about actually moving into the room?"

"We've come this far," she said, liking him more by the second. "We might as well go all the way."

His left brow rose and she realized her double entendre. "Go call room service."

"I will in a moment," he said. "But first, there's something I need to do." He took her coat and laid it over one of the wing chairs. His own coat followed. Then his suit jacket.

Her eyes widened at the contrast between his shoulders and his hips. And when he turned she got a nice long look at his behind, which was as stunning as anything she'd seen in ages. She wanted to touch it. Run her hand along the curve.

He turned, walked up to her, lifted her chin with the side of his finger until she met his gaze. Then, slowly, he bent and kissed her.

Her eyes fluttered shut as she felt the tenderness of his lips. It was a soft kiss, a brush, barely touching. Puff of breath, and she could taste him, breathe him in, and she leaned in, wanting more.

He obliged, but in his own time. "Susan," he whispered against her lips. Then a soft, cool kiss that lingered, deepened as the seconds ticked by. As the night changed from question to promise.

Pressing harder, he used his lips to open hers, then his tongue flicked once, twice against the soft inner flesh under her top lip. Her gasp gave him full entrance, and he took advantage of the situation. Now he explored her more fully, not rushing, languid, as if he needed to learn every taste, every nuance.

She put her hand on his neck as she did her own exploration. Teasing heat and a flavor that was completely new. Completely David. Her fingers moved up into his hair, and she could hardly believe how soft, how smooth. She moaned as his arm went around her waist and he pulled her tight against him, and when he shifted his hips, she felt his hard length press her lower belly.

She shivered at the contact, at the heat. He thrust into her mouth, and she captured his tongue, sucking hard. It was his turn to moan.

His arm stayed around her waist, although he loosened his hold. His eyes were half closed, lazy with desire. She could see herself with him, in the bed, naked and touching and doing everything that pleasure would allow.

But that wasn't her plan. If she didn't do something about it now, she would be lost. This was her party, and she was going to keep it that way.

As he moved to take her mouth once more, she leaned back and shook her head. "Champagne," she whispered.

He looked into her eyes, letting her know he wasn't through.

He let go of her waist and walked to the phone by the couch. The thick outline of his cock pushed against the fine wool of his pants. As he spoke to room service, he turned away, and she felt a flush on her cheeks as she realized he'd watched her checking him out.

Luckily, her desire wasn't so obvious. It was the only thing that made her plan workable. If he had any idea what he did to her...

She grabbed her purse and made a dash for the bathroom. Locking the door behind her, she leaned against the cold wood and exhaled a breath she hadn't realized she'd held.

This was unbelievable. Completely outside of her experience. She'd been with a few other men. Men she wasn't in love with. A long time ago she'd come to terms with her sexuality. She liked it hard, fast, uncomplicated. But this...

This was thrilling. Seductive. Erotic as all get-out.

Pushing herself off the door, she went to the sink, where she fixed her makeup and brushed her teeth, using the time to calm her racing heart. Although she wasn't very successful at that, she was able to map out the next few steps.

The champagne would arrive, they'd talk. Not touch. She needed him pliant, obedient. After seeing his erection, she was pretty sure that wouldn't be a problem.

Then she would begin. She'd make it an evening neither of them would forget.

When she went back into the sitting room, David stood by the window, looking down at the traffic below. He'd loosened his tie, but hadn't taken it off.

Slowly, he turned from the window, his face pensive, questioning.

"What's that look?" she asked.

"Just thinking."

"About?"

"Us."

"Go on."

"I don't feel any hesitation about this. Which is odd. I mean, we're strangers. We don't even know each others' names. You could be—"

"Anyone. I know."

"But not really. We can only be who we are."

She walked across the room until she was very close to him. "Ah, but that begs the question, who are we, really? Are we the same person with the lights out? With a stranger on the fifteenth floor?"

"I don't know the answer to that."

"I don't either. It's going to be interesting to find out."

He studied her face intently, looking at everything—her forehead, her cheeks, her chin. "I think we all have many natures. Some much darker than we'd care to admit."

Her hand went to his face and she traced a line down his jaw. His skin felt warm and smooth. He must have shaved recently. Her exploration was good, but it wasn't enough. She found herself wanting to taste him, to lap his face like a grooming cat.

"Why did that make you smile?"

"A rogue thought," she answered. "Actually, I think it's true. We do have our darker selves. I don't mean evil, although I suppose that's part of it, too. I mean wicked. Desires we'd never admit to another soul for fear they would run away in horror. Or at the very least never invite us to another cocktail party."

His grin changed his face. Made him all the more accessible, but a moment later, his face grew solemn again. "What if you could tell someone those thoughts? What if you knew, completely and without reservation, that there would be no bad consequences. You wouldn't be shunned, or made to feel guilty, or wicked. What if it was all okay?"

She took in another deep breath, then let it out slowly. "It might be very exciting."

He nodded.

"And very fulfilling."

He nodded again.

"But scary, too."

His brows arched slyly. "That's the point, isn't it?"

Her response was cut off by a knock. She gave him a "stay put" look and headed for the door, trying to walk as if her whole body wasn't trembling. The waiter was mercifully efficient, and in short order she was alone with David, each of them holding a crystal glass filled with a very good vintage of Dom Perignon.

"To desire," David said, touching his glass to hers.

"To desire." And then she sipped the chilled bubbly, savoring the taste and the moment. It was, as they say on Broadway, show time.

THE MOST EXTRAORDINARY THING about the moment, David realized, was that he was more aroused than any other time in his thirty-two years, and yet he was still able to hold a glass. Smile. Speak in complete sentences.

But his luck wasn't going to hold out forever. Everything in him wanted to take charge, to make her his. But he also knew she didn't want that. Not yet, at least. In this tango, she was leading, and that alone had him hot and bothered. He'd never been with a woman quite like Susan. More than ever, he was confident that his first impression of her had been accurate. She came from strength, from wealth. Her confidence was sexy, and the way her eyes fairly danced with possibilities nearly drove him over the edge.

He couldn't wait to see what she would do. Undress him? Top him? Damn, he'd never done that before. A lot of his clients were into being dominated. The more successful, the more likely they were to want the release of someone else taking control, at least in the bedroom. He'd heard stories, knew the lingo, had had himself a fantasy or two.

There was no doubt if she was into domination, she'd be damn good at it. He pictured her in black leather. With all that blond hair, it was almost too good. Then his fantasy lifted and he saw her as she was. Goddamn, she was gorgeous. Her hair was up in another clip, and his fingers itched to let it loose. Her dress showed off her curves, her legs. He especially loved the high heels.

She slipped the champagne glass from his hand and put it down on the coffee table, then led him to the bedroom. He liked it. The size, the headboard. Oh, yeah.

"Lie down," she whispered.

He went for his tie, but she stopped him.

"Just as you are."

He didn't think to question her. Hell, at this point if she asked him to stand on the bed and recite the National Anthem, he would have.

He chose the side farthest from the bathroom. Women liked being closer. As she clicked off the overhead light, he climbed on the bed, on his back, his hands underneath his neck.

The only illumination was from a lamp on the far side of the room. It was enough. He could see her clearly, read the anticipation in her eyes. Next time, they'd do it his way. With the lights on. But tonight, shades of gray seemed appropriate.

She walked to the foot of the bed and removed his shoes, putting them neatly on the dresser. His penis twitched, wanting very much to be released. The constriction had just gone from slight discomfort to acute distress.

She moved to the other side of the bed, but she didn't sit down. She didn't do anything more than look at him for what felt like minutes, but might have been seconds. "Move to the middle of the bed," she said, finally.

"The middle?"

She nodded. And waited.

He obeyed, positioning himself in the center of the exceptionally large mattress.

She seemed satisfied. Yet she still didn't make a

move to take off her clothes, or his. "Do you know the real story of Scheherazade?" she asked him, her voice as seductive as any siren.

"I know about the thousand and one nights."

"Ah, that's the other version. The G-rated version."

"Okay," he said, wondering where this was heading. Role-playing? He guessed he could do that. Depending on whom she wanted him to be.

"You see," she continued, "Scheherazade didn't really tell stories about magic lamps or cunning sailors. At least, not the stories in all the books. Her tales were far more...erotic."

Susan leaned over the bed, touched her lips to his in a teasing kiss. He flicked his tongue, but she pulled back. Shaking her head, she said, "Naughty."

He groaned his frustration, but she didn't seem to care. She took his lips again with the same feathery touch. He breathed her in, her scent intoxicating, dangerous. When she slipped his tie off, he couldn't hold still another moment. He touched her hair with one hand, the back of her neck with the other. He wanted her near him, naked, with that mane of blond hair splashed across the pillows.

He wasn't going to get it. She stepped away, sighed, then went to the dresser. Instead of putting down his tie, she held on to it while she went into her purse. He couldn't see what it was she held in her hands as she headed back to the bed.

"I can see that you're going to need a little help," she said.

He looked down at his pants. The strain was almost too much. The seams could go any second.

She chuckled, a rich, deep sound that made him clench his muscles. ''Not with that. At least, not yet.'' She took his hand in hers, turned it palm up and placed gentle kisses on the tips of his fingers. It was nice, but—

Her mouth sucked in his index finger, all the way. The hot wet velvet made him squirm. Impossible to lie still and endure this incredible torture.

The next second, her mouth was gone. His hand was drawn up and out, and he realized that she was going to tie him to the bed. His whole body shifted into fourth gear, as if he'd been idling for the past hour, and now he was on the field, ready for the race. Although the idea of being helpless this soon in the game sent off warning signals.

His tie circled his wrist gently. He tested the hold, and found it was insubstantial; he could pull free in a moment. His worry dissipated, at least partly. She wanted the choice to be his. Did he want to pull free? Or did he want to enter her world?

The resounding answer was that he wanted very much to get on with it. And the only reason it felt safe to plunge ahead was *because* he could escape. Because she had understood that this journey was as much of the mind as the body.

She used something else to tie his left wrist. A scarf. When she was through, he sighed deeply, strangely at peace. At least he understood part of the game. He wasn't to move. Until she let him.

The bed dipped as she climbed up next to him, on

her knees. Then one leg went over his hips, and she straddled him, the juncture of her thighs lying directly on top of his erection.

"Now," she said. "We can begin."

His eyes closed as he dragged in a gasping breath. He couldn't come. Not yet. Not like this.

It took all his will, all his strength to calm himself down as the heat of her seeped inside his pants. An ember, he'd wager, that would turn into a bonfire before the night was through.

4

SO MANY CHOICES. He was her very own buffet, and she could nibble to her heart's content. Unbutton his shirt? She'd like to see his chest. On the other hand, maybe she should ignore the shirt and go directly to the pants.

While she pondered her delicious decision, she ran her hands over his arms, his chest. His body tensed, but he stayed in position. From his quiet struggle, she could see he wasn't familiar with this role. He liked to be in charge.

Not tonight. And to reinforce the fact, she moved her hips back and forth, pressing herself against his straining erection. His moan was almost as satisfying as his expression. All that restrained lust made her tremble. Damn, this was fun.

"Shall I tell you what I want?" she asked, knowing he would say yes. In his condition, he would have agreed to anything.

He nodded. Opened his mouth, then closed it again, along with his eyes. A muscle twitched in his jaw, and his hands grasped his restraints as if they were lifelines.

She wondered how long it would take for him to lose it. For a moment, she pondered taking pity on the man. Undoing his belt, perhaps. No. The point of this little excursion was to set the tone. To see if her plan would work.

"I want," she whispered, as she leaned over to touch the hollow of his throat with her fingers, "to play."

His eyes snapped open and she took the challenge, her gaze and his locked. "I want to be anybody," she said. "Anybody I've ever dreamed of being. I want to take out each one of my wicked desires, one at a time, and see where they take me. Take us."

"Oh, God."

She smiled. "I'll interpret that as interest?"

"Yes." The word was thick, low. As if his body were doing too many other things to be bothered with speech. Which, she imagined, was the truth.

She moved her hands down his chest again lightly, feeling him quiver beneath her. When she reached his belt, she toyed with the buckle, knowing she was driving him nuts, and loving it. "And I want you to whip out your—"

He inhaled sharply.

"...fantasies. No hesitation. No embarrassment. Tonight, dear David, is a prelude. A summit of sorts. We'll lay the ground rules. There are lots of things I want to try, but there are certain taboos."

"For example?"

She hesitated. Her voice had been steady all the way through her little speech. Confident, in fact. As if she did this every night. But now she was about to cross the line. Tell him things she'd never told anyone before. Not even Larry. If it was awful, if she hated it, she would never have to see David again. She hoped it wasn't awful. "I'm not excited by cross-dressing," she said.

"Me cross-dressing, or you?"

"Both. I like the differences between us."

He flexed his shoulders, but he didn't let go of the ties. "Go on."

"I don't like pain. Well, not a lot of pain."

"What does that mean?"

She leaned down and captured his right nipple between her teeth. It would have been more interesting had he been undressed, but she could still make her point. She held the hard nub gently, flicking her tongue over the silk of his shirt. Then she increased the pressure.

His back arched as she continued to bite him. When he hissed and bucked slightly, she let him go.

He settled back down, squirmed, letting her know her illustration had had far-reaching effects, and met her gaze again. "I see."

"Good. Now it's your turn."

"You're done? Those are the only two things you don't like?"

"No. But it's still your turn."

After exhaling and flexing his hands a few times, he nodded. "I don't like it *too* messy. No unexpected bodily fluids."

"Well said."

"I try."

"Go on."

"I don't care to enlarge the circle."

"Hmm. Now that's unusual."

"What?"

"Most men would sell a lung to be with two women at the same time."

"Nope. I like to focus. I don't want any distractions."

"So, I should call Tom Cruise and cancel?"

"Hey, no fair. I didn't know you were going to ask *him*."

She laughed. It took an exceptional man to be humorous when the subject was another man.

"I believe it's your turn again," he said.

"Right." She let her hands wander south, and this time when she hit his belt, she kept going. Her touch as light as a feather, she ran her fingers down the straining length. "Safety first. No risking anyone's life."

"Good plan."

"And we'll always have an out. A safe word. I don't want any psychological scarring here. This is meant to be freeing. Not twisted."

His hips pushed up, his desperation mounting. There was more to be said, but first she needed to show a bit of mercy.

"David," she said softly.

He grunted an attempt at a reply.

"We're not going to have sex tonight."

His groan was achingly heartfelt.

"Because we both need to think this through. This is new territory. Risky business. We're going to be vulnerable. Bare our throats, as it were."

"Susan," he said, forcing the word out between clenched teeth. "I appreciate what you've said. And

I concur. However, you should understand that I'm going to die in about two minutes. And all your hard work will be in vain.''

''Hmm. I suppose you have a point.''

''To say the least.''

She laughed again, but as she did, she lifted herself to her knees, her back straight, her eyes locked on his. Her hands went to the back of her head where she opened the tortoiseshell clip. Her hair tumbled around her shoulders and down her back.

David's mouth opened and his cheeks flushed with color. She knew he'd react this way. The next step was going to be even more fun.

Slowly, knowing he couldn't have looked away if he was on fire, she shook her head, fanning the last of the kinks from her hair. Only then did she lower her body once more. Controlling her movements with her thighs and her hips, she rode him. Friction, tension and heat were all focused on about eight inches of thick flesh. Her own breath became shaky as she rubbed harder, and she had to shift her position so she got as well as she gave.

''Oh, my God,'' he said, thrusting up to meet her. ''I can't... Please...''

''Please what?''

''I need to touch you.''

''You are touching me.'' She squeezed her thighs to remind him of the contact.

''No. It's not enough. Let me touch you. I need to feel your skin. Your hair.''

''But that would mean untying you.''

He groaned pitifully.

She increased her pace. Even though she wanted to feel his arms, his hands, she wasn't going to give in. Like Scheherazade, she was going to hold back. Keep an ace in the hole. She wanted this to work. She wanted a playground, and she wanted her anonymity, and she wanted it with him.

His breathing changed, and she knew he was close. She bore down hard and ground herself against him. He wasn't the only one close. Oh, damn, she was going to come before he did. No, no. Not yet. Not yet...

Her body shuddered violently as she climaxed. Tremors from deep within stole her breath. She arched her back as she continued to ride him. David moaned and thrust his hips up hard, and then every muscle in his body tensed as he passed the point of no return. His head went back, his neck bare and straining as he gritted his teeth. She wanted to stay, to watch him come down, to see the release in his eyes, but that wasn't for tonight.

She slipped off the bed, grabbed her purse and her coat, and ducked into the bathroom. One coat of lipstick and a surprise for him, then she hurried to the door. Although she shouldn't have, she looked back. David had gone slack, his chest heaving with his efforts to cool down.

When his head started to turn, she slipped out, closing the door behind her.

Walking on shaky legs to the elevator, she congratulated herself on a job well done. She'd actually pulled it off. No strings, no names, no boundaries. What could be more enticing?

The elevator door opened and she settled next to a nice-looking man in his forties. He tried not to stare, but his gaze kept coming back to her. Was it her hair? Men did love her hair. Or was it the look of smug satisfaction she couldn't quite tame?

It didn't matter. She'd done it. She'd gone after what she wanted. Not that it was a replacement for love and marriage and all that. She'd date if someone interesting came along. This was about pleasure. About breaking the rules. About knowing exactly why he was with her.

When the elevator hit the lobby, she gave her staring friend her most dazzling smile, then headed for home. She couldn't wait to get into bed. What dreams she'd have tonight.

"SUSAN?"

When she still didn't answer, David sighed. She'd disappeared. Why? It had all gone her way. So why ditch him? Why go to all this trouble and not even have sex? Okay, so they'd had sort-of sex, and he had to admit, he'd come like Old Faithful, but still. He hadn't touched her once.

The thought reminded him about the ties around his wrists and in short order he'd freed himself. She'd left her scarf. If he knew her name, he would return it to her.

Dammit. Why the tease? How had he been so wrong about her? It made no sense.

He got up, stretched his neck muscles a bit, then headed for the bathroom. As he walked in, he smelled her perfume, the scent as mysterious as the woman.

Something in the mirror caught his eye and he looked at the opposite wall. Nothing. He went to the sink, and the explanation was simple. It wasn't reflected on the mirror. It was on the mirror itself. A message. In scarlet lipstick.

NEXT WEDNESDAY.

He grinned. She hadn't ditched him. She'd just left in a very unique way. But then, this whole night had been unique. She was something else. Someone he wanted to discover.

God, what would her fantasies be? He felt pretty confident they weren't going to be run-of-the-mill. He just hoped he was up to the task. A shudder hit him as he remembered the feel of her on top of him, the way she rubbed him so sensuously it was all he could do not to explode in the first two minutes.

How in hell was he going to live through next week?

Getting down to the business at hand didn't distract him from his thoughts. As he washed up, it occurred to him that he was fifty percent of this duet. He'd have to come up with some ideas of his own.

Her tied up, spread-eagle, on the bed.

Okay, so that wasn't terribly original. So what. He wasn't trying to reinvent the wheel.

Him, on his knees, spreading her open before his eager mouth.

He grabbed the towel off the rack and dried his face.

He had seven days to get through. His patients deserved his full attention. Charley and Jane had rescheduled dinner for tomorrow night. His sister, Karen, was coming in for lunch on Monday. It was imperative that his primary focus be his regular life. At night, when he was safely in bed, he could think about…this. Fantasize to his heart's content.

But not during business hours. He stared at his reflection, making sure he understood that he was serious. Then he dried himself off and headed out.

By the time he got to the elevator, he was hip deep in a scenario that could best be described as sex on wheels. Susan. Him. Back seat of a limo.

Shit.

The elevator arrived. He stepped inside, smiled at the elderly gentleman to his left, and wondered if it was time for him to go back and see his own shrink.

BY THE TIME Susan got to the theater, Peter and Andy were pacing in front of the box office. The play was by Nicky Silver, who was a favorite of hers, and the star was Peter Frechette, one of the best actors she'd ever seen. The night promised to be delightful, complete with après performance with the cast. And yet, Susan wanted to be somewhere else. Home, to be exact. It wasn't that she didn't love her friends, after all, Peter had been part of the gang since day one back in college, and he'd always been there for her, but in the two days since her evening with David, she'd barely been able to string two coherent thoughts together.

She felt like a voyager, setting off on an adventure filled with great risks, daring deeds, and possible treasure. Everything about David appealed to her, particularly that she knew virtually nothing about him. No family history, no comparative bank statements, no work baggage. He was elemental man, and he was hers for at least one more night. Wednesday had taken on all sorts of mythic proportions, and she'd giggled more than once at the very appropriate nickname of "hump day."

"About time," Peter said, scowling. He hated being late.

"I'm horrible. I don't know why you love me."

He rolled his eyes at Andy, his significant other. "I don't know why, either."

She brushed imaginary lint off his coat shoulder, then kissed him softly on the lips. "But you do love me. That's the point."

"Only because act one hasn't started. If you'd been five minutes later..."

"Well then, why are we standing out here? Let's go."

Andy laughed, took Peter's hand and led them inside the theater. It was an off-Broadway house, the Manhattan Theater Club, and they had season tickets.

After they found their seats, Susan got her Playbill and flipped through the pages. Not that she was reading it. She hadn't read much in the last two days. Or nights.

God, she was obsessed. She wished it was three weeks from now, and that she and David had settled into a routine. Nice, exciting, but not all-consuming. Sex. That's all. Just sex and fun with a gorgeous guy. Everyone needs a hobby, right?

"Susan."

She turned to Peter. "Hmm?"

"What is with you?"

"Pardon?"

"You're being very weird. Is there something you want to tell me?"

"Weird? Moi? I don't think so."

Peter turned to Andy. Although she couldn't see him, she knew he'd rolled his eyes again. Peter was quite fond of that gesture. When he turned back to her, his gaze went straight to her, no rolling, no mocking. Maybe a little bit of worry.

"I'm fine. Preoccupied, but fine."

"Preoccupied about what?"

"Nothing important."

Peter sat up straighter. "A man. This is about a guy, isn't it?"

"No," she said. Perhaps too loudly, as the couple in the seats in front of her turned to give her the evil-theater stare. "No," she said again, whispering this time. Wondering why she was lying. Peter would understand. All her friends would. Maybe. If she told them.

"I don't believe you, sweetheart." Peter took her hand in his. "So I'll just pretend you said yes. I hope he's good enough for you. And that he doesn't give one damn about, you know."

She nodded. Leaned toward telling him all. Asking his opinion. But then the house lights dimmed and her decision was put off for the next couple of hours.

By the time the play had ended and the three of them headed backstage, she'd changed her mind. For now, at least. David was hers. She didn't want opinions, or cautions, or even raised eyebrows.

She didn't even want encouragement, which was confusing but true.

As they waited their turn to congratulate the playwright, she watched Peter and Andy. They'd been together over a year. Peter, who was a marvelous actor himself, had fallen for the man after getting reacquainted at a friend's wedding. The two of them had first met in college, but things hadn't worked out then.

Now, they seemed blissful. Truly content with each other. Andy wasn't glamorous, or the best-looking guy on the block. But he was kind, and funny, and the way he treated Peter made her want—

Yes. Okay. Despite her hedonistic attitude toward the stranger named David, she did want to be part of a couple. And who knows? Maybe, one day, she'd find her other half.

In the meantime, there was no reason she couldn't have a good time. Many good times.

She closed her eyes and pictured David. Particularly his luscious lower lip. It was only Friday. Many, many days to go before Wednesday. Thank God she had to work on Monday. That would help. Tuesday, however, would be completely focused on wardrobe selection, hair removal, facial and fantasy selection.

A tremor shot down her back as heat filled her cheeks. Luckily for her, Nicky Silver turned to her just then, and she could pretend her flushed demeanor was because of the play.

When she'd finished their brief talk, she found Peter staring at her. "This is someone different," he said. "Isn't it?"

She opened her mouth to deny it, but even she couldn't tell that bold a lie. "Yeah."

"Are you being safe?"

She shrugged. "Depends on what you mean by safe."

"I'll settle for physically at the moment."

"Then yes."

"I'm here," he said, taking her hand. "We're all here for you. Any time."

"I know. And I love you for it."

"Love him later," Andy interrupted with a grin. "I need dinner."

5

DAVID LEANED BACK in his chair, debating dessert. Jane would order her usual chocolate cake, and Charley would shake his head and ask for black coffee. When the sinfully rich cake arrived, Charley would take one bite, then another. He usually ate the lion's share. But in his interestingly warped mind, because he didn't order it, he didn't have to feel guilty about it.

"We're doing Lamaze on Wednesday nights," Jane said, turning to David even as her hand went to Charley's shoulder. The two of them were the best example of a happy marriage he'd ever seen, and David was proud of his part in getting them together.

Only a year ago Jane had been a rather anonymous employee at Charley's firm, when she'd been struck by a falling plaster cupid, of all things, which disrupted her memory. She'd believed she was Charley's fiancée, and David had nurtured the misconception. As he'd hoped, Jane worked her magic on his stuffy friend, and they'd ended up together.

Unfortunately, David wasn't so adroit with his own personal relationships. Not that he didn't want to be married. He did. He just wasn't willing to settle. Granted, he'd known some great women. Women with style and substance. But something had been lacking.

His sister Karen claimed he was too picky. But when he looked at Jane and Charley, he knew he was just being smart. He wanted what they had. He just hoped he wouldn't have to wait for another plaster cupid to fall from the sky.

"David?"

He smiled at Jane. "Yes?"

"What's going on? I don't believe you heard a word I said."

"You're going to Lamaze on Wednesday nights."

She frowned with her startlingly lush red lips. Despite marriage and pregnancy, Jane still managed to look like a child at times. With her blond curls, her pale face and wide, expressive eyes, she could fool the uninitiated into thinking she was the soul of innocence. David knew better. Behind those fluttering eyelashes was a savvy, mature woman who was the best thing that ever happened to Charley. "I also said that we should change our dinner dates to Thursdays."

He took a sip of coffee to hide his grin. If he had been the type to believe in signs and omens, he'd be pretty impressed. They'd had their Wednesday-night dinners for almost a year, and he'd dreaded asking them to change plans. "Thursdays are great. But on the third Thursday of the month, I have therapy group until seven. So I'll be a little late."

Jane nodded slowly, but her concentration didn't seem focused on dinner arrangements. "What's going on?'' she asked again, no sign of teasing in her voice this time.

"What do you mean?" Dammit, he shouldn't have looked away.

"Something's going on, and you know it." She leaned forward over the white tablecloth. "Come on. Spill."

David looked at Charley, who shrugged helplessly. "You're on your own, buddy."

"Thanks. Some friend you are."

"I want to help. Honestly. But once she gets going…"

"Yeah." David knew. Only, he didn't want to tell them about Susan. Not yet, at least. Maybe not ever. This was something private. Personal. He'd never kept secrets from Charley, not in all the years they'd been friends. But something about this…assignation was different. "Nothing's going on, Jane," he said as he signaled the waiter.

"I don't believe you." Jane touched his hand and made him look right at her. "I think you're into something, and it's a fairly large deal. And I'd bet the moon it has everything to do with a woman."

David didn't blink. Not once. But the second the waiter appeared he ordered an apple tart, more coffee, then excused himself to visit the men's room.

He'd never admit it to Charley, but sometimes Jane scared him. But not in a bad way. She was just too…Jane.

SUSAN SCOWLED at her image in the mirror. She hadn't worn this dress in a long time, and now she remembered why. It made her ass look like a double-wide trailer.

She stripped, but she didn't put the dress on the bed with the dozen other discarded outfits. This one went on the giveaway chair.

She was no longer amused.

She'd been trying on clothes for hours, and nothing, *nothing,* was right. In forty minutes, she had her facial, then her manicure and pedicure. She still hadn't shaved her legs, and she had to wash her hair and do her makeup and, dammit, why was there always so much grooming involved?

Maybe her fantasy should be about hobos.

She sighed as she went back to the closet. Staring blindly at the rows of dresses, skirts and blouses, it hit her again that tonight wasn't a dress rehearsal. It was the real deal.

Tonight could be the first of who knows how many erotic nights spent with the delectable David. Or it could be a fiasco of epic proportions. She voted for the former.

But, in order for things to work out smoothly, she needed to prepare. She had to pick something to wear. It was a bit early in the game for her to show up naked under a trench coat. She grinned, as she filed that mental memo under *Future Plans.*

She could just wear anything, a suit, her red Prada, even jeans. But she wanted more. She wanted to set the tone. It was only fair, after all. If this worked out, David would have ample opportunities to delve into his fantasies and take the reins, but tonight was hers. She needed to do this. She needed to see if she could walk the walk, not just talk the talk.

Which led her right back to her indecision. Not just about her outfit, but about her fantasy du noir. Now that she had the time, the man, the ground rules, what was she going to do with them?

Not that she didn't have fantasies she wanted fulfilled. On the contrary—she had too many.

Bondage? Well, maybe. But not yet. That required a whole new level of trust. Although she had to admit, she'd loved tying him up last week. He'd looked good enough to eat, all helpless and hard. Next time, she wouldn't leave his bindings so loose. Next time, she'd make sure he stayed where she put him.

And next time, he'd be naked.

She pulled out a black Versace, the one that fit like a second skin. Actually, more like a girdle, which was great when she went to a cocktail party, but it was a demon to take off.

As she put the dress back, an image swam up. Her wrists tied. Her body at his disposal, unable to stop him if he, say, chose to lick every exposed inch of skin.

She shivered at the idea. She'd never pictured herself in that way. Control was too big an issue. But this wasn't about control, was it? This was about letting go. Freeing herself, exploring her boundaries.

But not tonight. Tonight was about building trust, about communication.

Role-play? Maybe. She'd always had a thing about

policemen, but for that they'd need costumes and props and she didn't want to go there, yet.

She closed her eyes as she nudged her subconscious to kick it up a notch. She could do anything—be anyone! So what was her problem?

Perhaps she was trying too hard. Yes. That was undoubtedly the problem. There was a great deal to be said for spontaneity. Once they were together, once they'd gotten past the first kiss, inspiration would strike. Of course it would.

The only thing she needed to decide was how far she wanted the sex to go. Kissing, absolutely. Hell, one of her recurring fantasies was to make out with a dream date for hours on end. But she was too anxious to pull that off. She wanted to see him. All of him. And she wanted him to see her.

Just then her gaze hit on a black dress she'd had for three years. Strapless, with a form-fitting bodice, it didn't look like much on the hanger. And even when she had it on, it wasn't spectacular. But that was sort of the point. She wanted him to notice *her,* not her dress. Once she added jewelry, the right shoes, black stockings…

She pulled the dress on and went to the full-length mirror. Eyeing herself critically, she nodded. In a perfect world, her boobs would have been bigger, her waist smaller, but seeing as how there was no time for major surgery, this was it. Now, she'd better get it in gear. The clock was ticking.

SEVEN-FIFTY, and Susan still had no idea what she was going to do with David. If he showed up. No, he would show up, with expectations of a wildly inventive, erotic night.

She glanced over her shoulder, then turned back to her drink. Jay, the bartender, made a perfect martini and for that she was grateful. The delectably attractive man also had the rare gift of silence. No idle chitchat, even though she was the only patron in the bar.

She sat up straighter on the leather stool, pulled her skirt lower on her thigh. Something made her turn again to the door, perhaps a sound, maybe a shift in the air.

David stood just inside the bar, his camel coat almost as elegant as he was handsome. Her stomach contracted in a completely sexual reaction as a frisson shot down her back making her breath hitch and her toes curl.

It had been a long time since she'd felt this way about a man. It made sense, purely on an aesthetic level. While David wasn't model-handsome, with features that could, by themselves, be considered ungainly, the totality of him worked in a major way. His height, his long, lean body. The bedroom eyes, his nose, bigger than it should be, yet just right. And then there were his lips. If they gave out awards for such things, he'd have shelves of trophies.

He smiled then, seeing her. She smiled back and with every step he took, her heart pounded harder. The way he looked at her didn't help the situation. His gaze was curious, hungry, wicked.

She should stop this. Right now. Let go of her fool-

ish idea of seduction and fantasy and get to know the man. The real man. And let him know her.

As quickly as the thought hit, she dismissed it. When would she ever learn? There was a difference between fantasies and fairy tales, and believing there was a chance for her and David to live happily ever after was a fairy tale, indeed. Better to stick with sex. With anonymity.

David reached her side, touched the back of her neck with cool fingers as he leaned down. His lips brushed her ear as he whispered, ''You're stunning.''

She shivered, as much from the conviction in his voice as the tickle of his breath, but waved the compliment away. His eyes narrowed as if with a question, but she pointed to the bar stool next to her before he could speak.

He sat, although he didn't seem very interested in ordering a drink. He focused on her. But it wasn't an ordinary look. It was more of an *experience.* Perhaps it was the intelligence in his gaze, or maybe just his energy, but there was something unique and thrilling about the way he studied her. It was as if she was the most fascinating person on earth, and he only had a few moments to memorize each detail.

''How come you're not married?'' she asked, surprised even as the words left her mouth.

He seemed surprised, too. ''I don't know.''

''I can't imagine you haven't had opportunities. With your looks, I'll bet they're pounding on your door.''

He laughed, totally unselfconsciously, a deep baritone tinged with self-deprecation. "I wouldn't say pounding."

"What would you say?"

"I'd say I don't want to talk about other women."

"Good answer."

"I try."

The tightness came back to her insides as he leaned over and kissed her lightly on the lips. His breath was warm and his lips cool, the contrast wonderful. He lingered, not increasing the pressure at all, just brushing his lips against hers, back and forth. It was an incredibly intimate gesture, more so than if he'd used his tongue to tease. It was all she could do to stay still, to let him explore in his own measured pace, let their breaths mingle until they became one breath.

Finally, he paused. She moved back a tiny bit and licked his lower lip as if it were a lollipop.

His sharp intake of breath pleased her. In fact, she wanted to do everything she could to make him do that again. To make his eyes widen with surprise.

He sat back, signaled Jay, then turned to her. "Can I get you another drink?"

She shook her head. "There's champagne in the room."

He nodded slowly. "About that. I don't know what arrangements you've made, but I want to take care of the bill."

She honestly didn't care who paid what, but, and she'd given this a lot of thought, she didn't want him finding out anything more about her. "Tell you what," she said. "The first time was my treat. From now on, we'll trade. I'll get it one Wednesday, you get it the next. And this Wednesday, we'll start with me.''

He considered her offer, and she thought he was going to protest until the two little worry lines between his eyebrows relaxed. ''Fair enough. My turn next week.''

She stuck out her hand. ''Deal.''

He took said hand, lifted it to his lips and kissed her softly. Without letting her go, his gaze met hers. ''I've thought of nothing but you for a week,'' he whispered.

The frisson came back, an electrical thrill that melted her doubts and revved her excitement. ''I know what you mean.''

''Do you?''

She nodded. ''I haven't been this nervous since last week.''

He grinned, but then his expression turned more serious. ''We don't have to do this,'' he said. ''You can change your mind any time.''

''Do you want to stop?''

''God, no.''

She had to smile. This was one cute guy. ''How about a cocktail?''

''God, yes.''

Jay arrived and David ordered a scotch. When the bartender went off to work his magic, she made a decision. When all else failed, she liked to try the truth. ''David?''

He shifted so he was facing her a bit more.

"Did you, uh, have anything in mind for tonight? Something in particular you wanted to do?"

His lips curled in a wry smile. "Oh, yes."

"Really?"

He nodded.

"And what would that something be?"

"Everything. Preferably all at once."

She laughed, surprised to find that she not only understood, but felt the same way. It wasn't that she wanted to try out new positions, or anything that mundane. She wanted to stretch her boundaries with him. She wanted to watch his expressions, hear him laugh and cry out. She wanted to see herself through his eyes. She'd never thought much about pheromones, but here was proof. She hardly knew the man, yet she was drawn to him in a way that defied logic.

"What about you?"

"Hmm?"

David touched her hand, and the touch was electric. "Did you have something in mind for tonight?"

She looked into his hazel gaze, wishing the lighting was a bit better so she could really see the color. She thought his eyes were more green than blue, but she couldn't be sure.

Jay came with David's martini, and after David paid the man, he turned back to Susan. "Sorry. I believe you were going to tell me about tonight?"

"I read an article a few weeks ago about fantasies," she said.

He sipped his scotch and she saw his hand wasn't

exactly steady. There was a slight tremor, which pleased her.

"Did you know that one of the most common, if not the most common fantasy among both men and women is to have sex with a stranger?"

"Really."

"It's true. And I think we qualify, don't you?"

"Are we still strangers?"

"Oh, my, yes."

"Even after last week?"

She nodded. "And we're going to keep being strangers if this is going to work."

"What do you think would happen if we got to know each other?"

"It wouldn't be this."

"This? What is this?"

His earnestness made her pause and think. "A man and a woman, deeply drawn to one another. Who want no inhibitions, no pressures from outside messing up what promises to be something very, very exciting."

"Fair enough," he said, but the way his voice cracked sort of spoiled his air of sophisticated indifference.

She smiled.

He smiled back. "Are we done here?"

"Yes," she said. "I believe we are."

It was almost show time. She still didn't know exactly how the night was going to proceed. Sex with a stranger, yes. But what kind of sex? Hard, fast, desperate? Slow exploration?

David ran his hand through his hair, and the gesture, common, insignificant, hardly worth a blink, gave her goose bumps. The way he picked up her coat made her blush. And when he touched the back of her arm, she trembled with anticipation.

Inspiration would come.

And so would she.

DAVID TOOK HER COAT from her shoulders, and headed toward the suite's corner table. He needed the mundane action to collect himself. The moment he'd seen her at the bar, he'd wanted to take her. And he wasn't particularly keen to be polite about it. But he needed to see where this was heading. No way he was going to blow this with his impatience, although, come on, he was only flesh and blood. And she had that pale skin. Blue, almost aqua eyes. Lips that could change a man's religion.

He lifted her coat briefly to his face. The outside of the heavy black garment smelled indifferent. Not unpleasant, just nothing distinguishing. Not like the inside. The inside smelled like her.

He closed his eyes as he inhaled, memorizing her scent. A hundred years from now, he'd recognize it, know it immediately as not just perfume, not only soap, but *Susan*. He tried to put words to the scent, but there weren't any. Nothing nearly accurate enough, nothing that said it was *this* smell and no other. But some part of him understood it was the scent of promise. Of daring. It was the scent of a woman who made him exceedingly grateful he was a man.

He placed her coat on the chair then covered it with his own. By the time he turned back to face Susan, she had moved next to the champagne bucket.

He needed to pour her a glass, himself one, too, but he didn't want to. What he wanted was to take her in his arms and kiss her until she wept. He wanted to throw her on the bed, and taste every inch of her body. He wanted to go crazy, and it was an effort to walk slowly, casually, as if there weren't coils of tension inside every muscle.

Susan held out her glass. He lifted the Dom Perignon, the same vintage as the last bottle, and filled her flute. He put the bottle back into the crush of ice, and watched her take her first sip. Red lips, full lips, caressing the cold impersonal edge of crystal.

He waited until she'd taken a few sips, then lifted the glass from her fingertips, captured the back of her neck with his palm, and took what he'd been wanting all night. Hell, all week.

He smoothed his lips over Susan's, nuzzling and nudging her mouth open for a long, melting kiss. She tasted of champagne, and she felt like the inside of heaven as he explored her at his leisure. She couldn't know that he wanted none of these niceties, that the last thing he wanted on earth was to take his time. Instead, he held himself strongly in check, and kept bringing himself back to the slick wet of her mouth, the searing heat of her tongue touching his, sucking his in a prelude that brought him from aroused to painfully hard in seconds.

He slipped his other arm around her waist and pulled her close, groaning as her breasts pressed against his chest. He wanted her naked. Naked and open and *his*. He wanted to do everything, taste her everywhere, make her scream and faint and rake his back with her nails.

The only hint of the madness inside him was when he moved his hips against hers, letting her feel his erection. She inhaled sharply. Good. So she understood. She knew that this was all for her. This restraint. Because if he'd had his way, she would already be screaming.

6

Susan felt the raw energy of David's desire through his lips, his hands, and from the heat pressed against her. She nipped his lower lip before she pulled back. He held her tighter for a moment, then let her go with a disappointed sigh.

After turning away, she shivered with her sense of power. Like Wonder Woman. If Wonder Woman even had a sex life. With that costume? *Oh, yeah.* She probably did it with a super hero and when they came, the bed exploded.

"This *everything* you want to do," she said, keeping her tone casual, as if she were asking about his summer vacation plans. "Are there any specifics?"

She heard him clear his throat, take a deep breath and release it slowly. Then his voice, soft and husky and patient. "Many."

She turned to him, noticing first the yearning in his gaze, then the still sizeable bulge in his pants. She must remember to use this power only for good. "Tell me."

A blush tinged his cheeks. "Tell you all of them?"

She hid her grin with the glass. "One to start with should be fine."

"Oh. Okay."

She handed him his champagne, and he took a long sip. "Well, uh…"

A valiant effort was unfolding before her. A man so tight with need he could shatter his glass forcing himself to think, to speak, to walk to the window. "Hmm."

"What?"

He turned to look at the city. "This isn't easy."

"Talking about it?"

"Yeah. I don't know why. Fantasies are normal. There's nothing to be ashamed of."

"Speak for yourself."

He whipped around, but stopped as he saw her teasing smile. "Very cute."

"And yet, I won't let you off the hook."

He nodded. Narrowed his gaze in that studious manner, then looked out the window again. "Mostly, they're pretty mundane. Sleeping with the girl in high school I never got to touch. The odd celebrity."

"How odd?"

He laughed. "That's not what I meant."

"I know. But I still want to hear who these celebrities are. Mine are David Duchovny and the guy who plays Krycek."

"Really?"

She nodded. "Don't worry. If that's who yours are, I won't be shocked."

"I would be." He grinned.

"Relentlessly heterosexual, eh?"

"Card-carrying." He sipped his drink. "What about you?"

"Yep. Although I have had a curious thought once or twice."

"Hmm."

"Second time you've done that."

"Done what?"

"That 'Hmm.' It sounds suspiciously like doctor-speak for 'I think you need a whole team of psychiatrists.'"

He must have swallowed wrong because he went into a coughing fit. She started toward him, but he held up a hand. A moment later, he calmed down. "Sorry."

"You okay?"

"Fine."

"So let's go back to the topic of David's Fantasies, celebrity division."

"Ah. Okay. Well, let's see. Sandra Bullock. Julia Roberts. Nothing shocking."

"Both good choices. But come on. Confess. Isn't there someone who isn't so…nice? Someone a little dangerous, perhaps?"

"Like you?"

"Me?"

He nodded then came toward her, stopping at the edge of the couch. "I have a sneaking suspicion you're as clever as you think you are."

"Which is dangerous?"

"Absolutely. A clever woman who understands herself and her desires is perhaps the most dangerous creature on earth."

"Oh, come on. There are plenty of scarier things. Politicians, for example."

He laughed. Damn, but she liked the sound. "Not in this situation. Unless, of course, you're planning on staging a filibuster."

"Hadn't thought of that. Kinky."

"Oh, right. Do the words pot and kettle ring a bell?"

She nodded, giving him that one. "I'm really not that scary. Not here. Not with you."

"No?"

"The situation couldn't be safer."

"Because we don't really know each other?"

"And because we don't want anything more than we've agreed to."

"Sex?"

"If you want to call it that."

"What would you call it?"

"Erotica. Sensuality. A daring adventure. A wicked temptation. Need I go on?"

He stared at her for a long moment, shifted a bit, the color rising once more in his cheeks. "I just want you to know that if I don't, uh, meet your expectations tonight, it's only because you're driving me insane, okay? Once I'm used to the way you... are...things will improve."

"Do you mean the event happening at all, or the duration of said event?"

"Duration."

"So we'll concentrate more on foreplay. That should help."

He shook his head. "Darlin', all you have to do is stand there and it's foreplay."

She walked the short distance between them. Her

gaze found his and she touched the side of his cheek with her hand. "I think I chose very, very well."

"You were actively in the market?"

"On the contrary, no. You inspired this whole plan."

"I did?"

"Don't look so shocked. You're gorgeous."

The way he looked at her said more than words. He seemed stunned.

"Surely you know that."

"Uh…"

She kissed him where her hand had been, drinking in his scent. Hugo Boss, if she wasn't mistaken. And male. Undiluted male. "Forget I said a word."

"Pardon?"

"I mean it. Forget I said that. Men who know they're gorgeous are usually insufferable."

"As opposed to women who know?"

She sighed. "No. Women are, too."

"You're not. Insufferable, I mean. And you're definitely gorgeous."

"Thank you. But I put my looks into perspective a long time ago. When I realized it didn't matter. Pretty doesn't equal happy. It doesn't guarantee love."

"True. And it can be diminishing."

"Yes. It can."

"For what it's worth, it wasn't your looks that brought me here."

She quirked her brow.

"Okay, so that was part of it. But that's more a chemical reaction than anything else."

"So what did bring you here?"

"All of you. Your mind. Your daring. The sound of your laughter. The promise in your voice. And I'll be damned if you don't smell better than anything or anyone on the planet."

"Ah, David. If this is all an act, don't tell me, okay? Let me go on in my delusional splendor."

He kissed her softly. "It's not an act. At least, not a conscious one. I won't hurt you."

She believed him. To a point. He wouldn't hurt her if she kept her distance. If she played the game. If she didn't let herself become vulnerable. Which wasn't going to be easy. He was a charmer, this one. A seducer. And if she wasn't careful, she could turn him from a fantasy into a fairy tale. Which would spoil everything.

"Why so sad? Do you want to get hurt?"

She shook her head. "Oh, God, no. In fact—"

"What?"

"Nothing. Let's just pretend we're in Switzerland. Neutral territory. No one gets hurt."

"You are kinky. But I think I can pull off a Swiss accent."

She laughed again, her brief melancholy chased away by his humor and vulnerability. She rarely saw the combination, especially in one so attractive. There had to be a reason he'd never married. Men like him don't get to their thirties unattached. "Come on now. Stop avoiding the question. Fantasies, please. In detail."

"Hey, I've answered the question. Several times."

"Nope. I don't believe you. Not that you're lying. But you aren't telling me the whole truth."

"I'm not?"

"Everyone has a few really juicy fantasies. The kind that makes you pray that guardian angels are a myth, because if they knew what you were thinking you'd be hit by lightning."

"Oh. *That* kind."

She headed for his place by the window. As she passed him, she trailed one finger across the width of his shoulders. He straightened. And although she couldn't see from this angle, she was pretty sure it wasn't just his posture that stiffened. "Well?"

"How about you go first. Then I'll go."

She turned toward the view, but her gaze didn't see past the window. His image was in the glass, vivid, yet translucent against the backdrop of Manhattan. For a moment, she toyed with egging him on, but that wouldn't be fair. It was her party, and she'd made up the rules. "All right."

David's mouth opened. Or perhaps the more accurate phrase was his jaw dropped.

It was perfect, really. She could see him, read his expression and his reaction, while he believed she wasn't looking. It was worth the butterflies in her stomach, the flush that heated her cheeks just thinking about what she was going to tell him. She drained her glass, wishing it was the whole bottle. Not really. But some courage, artificial or not, would be most welcome.

"I have always fantasized," she began, struggling

to keep her voice steady and natural. "About being helpless."

"Go on," he said, softly, as if he was afraid he'd spook her.

"A captive. The man, he's someone who follows me, tracks me down, becomes obsessed." She swallowed, marshalling the guts to continue. "He drugs me and steals me away to his secluded home. While I'm still groggy, he...prepares me."

David swallowed hard, then whispered, "Prepares you?"

Oh, God. This wasn't easy. Especially the next part. David was turned on, that was evident, but she was about to enter murky waters. One man's turn-on is another's squick. But, if she chickened out now, the whole plan would fall apart. "He shaves me bare. Every last vestige of hair below the waist. It makes me feel terribly vulnerable."

"Go on." David moved another step closer.

"My hands, my feet are bound. Sometimes on the bed. Other times, bent over a table or on a chair." She studied David as he came close enough to touch. His eyes, while still fully dilated, had a dreamy, hypnotic look to them. His mouth hung slightly open, revealing slightly crooked white teeth, and his nostrils flared from his deep breaths. Her gaze traveled south. Oh, my. How impressive.

"Don't stop now," he said, his voice dripping with lust.

"He does everything to me. Things I've heard about but never experienced."

"Like?"

"He takes me in every possible way a man can take a woman."

David groaned. "Please tell me that's a fantasy you want to come true."

She turned to face him. To drink in the full effect of her fantasy. The man was fairly thrumming with desire. Something told her if she went on and really gave him the details, he'd come right there, without a touch. He wanted her answer. She made him wait. But not too long.

When she figured he was about to turn blue from holding his breath, she nodded.

The next second she was in his arms and his mouth was on hers and the kiss stole her breath and the last of her qualms. His hand slipped around her waist, pulling her tight against him, and this time when she felt his erection it was no gentle tease. It was a promise.

She found his tongue with her own and they dueled for supremacy. Although David came out the victor, she won, too, as his kisses fogged her senses, arousal braiding into the white haze of adrenaline. He kissed her as if he'd known her forever, as if he could read her desire as he would read a book. The thigh nudging between her knees was elegant proof of that and she arched against him shamelessly.

David's lips traced a moist line down her throat, lapping and nipping, marking her as his. "Please," he growled, his tongue dancing at the hollow of her neck.

"Please what?" she whispered, her fingers moving to his hair, holding him against her so he wouldn't stop. "What do you want, David? Tell me what you want."

David pulled back, straightened and met her gaze. He seemed almost feverish with his face flushed and his eyes wide and dark. "I want you naked."

Her fingers, still in his hair, closed into a fist. His small gasp should have made her let go, but what she wanted was another spine-melting kiss before she carried out his request.

Holding him steady, she touched her lips to his. No tongue, not yet. Just lips and teeth and gentle nips. She kept on teasing him, tasting him, until the hand around her waist pressed into her painfully. Releasing him, she stepped back, and after a momentary struggle, he let her go. "Ask me what *I* want," she whispered.

"Tell me."

"Make me naked."

He closed his eyes for a moment, and when he opened them again he lifted his hand to touch the clip that held her hair in a loose bun at the back of her head. But he must have changed his mind because his hands soon rested on her shoulders. He ran one fingertip down to her slight décolleté. "This is insanity."

"What is?"

"How much I want this moment to last. How quickly I want to move on."

"Can't have it both ways."

"Why not?"

She laughed. "As this is the first time, why don't we take it slowly. Work for it."

"Excellent advice." He kissed her softly as he reached behind her. She felt her zipper go down, the bodice loosen. He skimmed her back with the tips of his fingers, making every part of her shiver. Just this side of tickling her, her skin seemed hypersensitive, his every touch sending shockwaves down to her toes.

"Susan."

She hadn't realized she'd closed her eyes until she opened them again. He held her gaze, never releasing her from the trance his touch induced. She had no idea how she remained on her feet while this...this madness coursed through her veins.

"Susan, are you sure?"

She nodded, touched that he would ask when he was in such a state. To prove her point, she removed her dress, uncovering her chest. She'd worn her black lace bra, and from his moan, she gathered it met with his approval.

"You're exquisite."

She closed her eyes as she leaned her head back.

His warm breath on the top of her breasts made her sigh, and when his fingers traced lazy circles around her covered nipples, she put one hand on the window to steady herself. Briefly, she pondered closing the drapes but she had a feeling they would be moving into the other room very shortly.

His mouth closed over her right nipple, and even through the lace she felt his delicate lips, his teasing tongue. He didn't rush at all, even though she knew he was desperate.

Her hands went to his head and she held him gently. He nipped her, and even with the barrier of her bra, she broke out in goose bumps from head to toe.

"David," she whispered, straightening, opening her eyes.

He mumbled something, not moving an inch.

"Bedroom."

That got his attention. He stood straight, kissed her once, hard, on the lips, then took her hand. As they passed the ice bucket, he grabbed the champagne bottle by the neck without breaking his stride.

A moment later, it was her, him, champagne and a king-sized bed.

7

DAVID PUT THE BOTTLE on the bedside table, then turned on the small desk lamp. He couldn't take his eyes off the woman in front of him. Her dress gone, her hard nipples poking at the lace of her black bra, he'd never seen anything more erotic in his life. If he didn't do something soon, he was going to explode.

He'd come to terms with the fact that he wouldn't be able to hold out much longer. But her effect on him was so strong, he'd rebound quickly, and then he'd be able to take his sweet time.

For now, though, he had a job to do. Make her naked.

She sighed as his lips closed once more on her nipple. Tasting lace, he pulled her dress past her hips and let it pool by her feet.

Matching panties. Garter belt. Black stockings and high heels. *She* was his fantasy. Only one thing would make the picture absolutely perfect. He released her hair from the clip. Blond silk unfurled around her shoulders. Stepping back so he could see all of her, she shook her head, and he was done for.

"David?"

"Yes?"

"I've changed my mind."

His heart stopped. *No. No. Please no.*

"I want you to get naked."

With a surge of gratitude, he breathed again, a great lungful of air. "You're evil," he whispered.

"I know. Aren't you glad?"

He nodded as his fingers fumbled with his shirt buttons. When he couldn't get the last one undone, he yanked the damn thing right off, then dropped his shirt where he stood. Next came his slacks, and he had to be a bit more careful there not to snag anything that shouldn't be snagged. It killed him to look away, but unless he wanted to fall, he had to focus to take off his shoes and socks. Finally, he stepped out of his pants and faced her, his black silk boxers not doing a thing to hide his arousal.

"I love it that we're color coordinated."

For a moment he didn't understand, then he realized she meant black underwear. "I think we'd look even better in flesh tones."

She tossed her hair behind her shoulders, then reached back to the clasp of her bra. He stood very still as she took the garment off and let it fall from her fingers.

He gritted his teeth, struggling to keep himself under control. Her breasts were beautiful, full, not too large, with luscious pink areolas and long, jutting nipples. Her perfection seemed almost holy.

A movement distracted him—her fingers running down her abdomen, pausing at the band of her lacy panties. Then she pulled them down slowly, past her thighs, her knees, and she let go. A step with each high heel, and she stood before him, close enough to touch, like a blond goddess. A true blonde. The soft slim patch of curly hair at the junction of her thighs was as golden as the rest of her.

"David?"

He grunted. It was the best he could do.

"It's your turn."

He nodded, not knowing where to look. Her breasts? Her face? The curve of her hip? He decided on her face, her eyes, as he pulled his boxers over his straining erection, then let them fall until he could step out of them.

His hand went to his cock, briefly, just a touch to go with the heat of her stare. She made a small sound, a little gasp, and he couldn't be still another second.

Without knowing how, he was in front of her and his hands were on her waist, pulling her close. He kissed her, drinking her in, the sweet scent of her perfume drowning him in bliss. His hands moved up her back, awed by her silky skin, and when she put her cool palms on his hips he bucked, bringing them in contact from chest to knee.

He pulled back from the kiss to look at her lips. Kiss-swollen and as pink as her nipples, he couldn't help picturing what they would look like wrapped around his cock. The thought made him groan.

She smiled in that way of hers, knowing and slightly sinful. Then her hand moved between them and down, and when she touched him he cried out, the sensation so intense it was almost painful.

"Is this for me?" she asked, gripping him firmly in her palm.

He struggled for words, but they wouldn't come.

Instead, he kissed her his answer. He was hers, whatever she wanted. Anything.

As her tongue darted into his mouth, she moved her velvet grip over the length of him and when she got to the head, one finger dipped into the bead of moisture there. She let him go, and when he moaned his disappointment, she pulled back from his kiss.

She brought that finger to her lips, and tasted him. It nearly did him in. He pulled down the comforter, leaving white sheets and two pillows on the big bed.

"Subtle," she said, but she took the hint and lay down, her golden hair cascading around her.

He climbed next to her and cupped her face with his hands. Holding her steady, he kissed her again, and this time it was hard, almost bruising, and he couldn't have stopped if the sheets had caught fire.

He'd never wanted anyone this badly. It was all he could do not to spread her legs and thrust into her and not stop until he passed out. But some small spark of rational thought remained, and he curbed his impulse, choosing instead to run his hands down from her breast to her belly, caressing the curve of her waist, her hips, her sides, then lower still.

The pads of his fingers stroked softly along the vulnerable skin of her inner thighs. "Do you like me touching you, Susan?" he asked.

"Yes," she said, drawing out the word into a long hiss of satisfaction as he brushed the soft hair of her cleft. With patience he didn't know he had, he stroked her nether lips, coaxing her open.

She sighed with pleasure, but it wasn't enough.

"I want to hear you say it." He dipped the tip of

his middle finger into her opening, sliding the wetness out over her clitoris, tracing a circle of infinity around and around the hard bud, savoring the feel as it rose to his touch. He listened intently to her breathing as it changed, became shallower, more labored.

"I love you touching me, David."

He leaned down and kissed her again, still running his finger delicately inside her warmth, his movements insistent yet gentle. Finally, he was rewarded with her gasp, and the arch of her hips.

"Let me make you come," he whispered.

She didn't answer in words, just pushed her hips up toward his hand.

He nibbled on her neck as he continued to make her writhe, torn between tasting her and watching her pleasure change her face. Her moans escalated as her body responded in the most incredibly wanton fashion. Hips thrusting, breasts quivering with each deep breath, her lips parted as she sucked in harsh breaths.

She shifted and he pressed his mouth to the tender skin just below her ear. He sucked her flesh softly, stopping only to flick his tongue against the damp skin. She whimpered helplessly as one finger, then two glided into her.

He felt her stiffen. Her neck muscles grew taut, the whole feel of her changing with the prelude to climax. He leaned back so he could see her, careful to keep his thumb rubbing her clitoris even as his fingers plunged into her heat.

"Oh, please," she said, her voice as tight as her body, her plea unselfconscious, wild with expectation.

And then she spasmed around him, arching off the

mattress, her hands grabbing the sheets and nearly tearing them off the bed. He didn't stop, even as she trembled beneath him, as she moaned words he couldn't understand, as her breath came in great gasps.

He'd never seen anything more beautiful. This was what he was made for, to give this woman pleasure, to watch her as she climaxed, to fan the flames of her desire.

Finally, her hand touched his, and, reluctant as all hell, he stopped, letting her catch her breath, but his hand didn't stray far. He splayed his palm over her stomach, watching it rise and fall, the rhythm matching the heartbeat he felt as he pressed his lips to her neck.

"Oh, my… That was so…"

His laughter must have tickled her, if the small jerk of her head was any indicator. "You're welcome."

Susan turned to him as she collected herself. The look in his eyes was both tender and hot. She felt as loose-limbed as a Raggedy Ann. "Umm, whatever can I do to thank you?"

Her hand went to his erection, and he gasped at the contact. Her soft palms moved up and down the length of him, gripping him just tightly enough. Then, as he fell back on the pillow, unable to hold himself steady, she leaned over him, kissing him once, gently, on the lips.

She paused, brought her hand to her mouth and licked her palm, moistening it from just above the wrist. David's eyes widened with lascivious bliss and he caressed her cheek in thanks. As she returned to her ministrations, she continued her exploration of his body, determined to taste every part of him she could reach.

Starting with the tip of his squared jaw, she nibbled and licked her way down his long throat, stopping a moment at the hollow of his neck. His scent filled her, rich and masculine, clean and sexy. She shifted on the bed, sitting to free her other hand. There was no way she could resist touching his chest. Firm and lightly peppered with light brown hair, she reveled in the feel of him, his soft skin encasing hard muscle just beneath. When she brushed his nipple, she was rewarded with a sharp intake of breath.

Sensitive. Some men weren't. But the way David arched his back, begging for more, gave her several ideas. She wasn't going to be rushed, however, and she licked his collarbone on her way to the side of his neck. She found the perfect spot under his ear, and followed her whim to bite him. Not hard. Well, not too hard. His yelp made her grin before she sucked him right there, wanting to mark him, to make him think of her every time he looked in the mirror.

His hand went to the back of her head, not protesting, simply touching her, making a connection. She released him from her hungry lips, then wandered down to his chest. Butterfly kisses all over his pecs, then her tongue circled his right nipple, not touching the hard peak.

As she predicted, he arched again. She prolonged his torment to lap at the tender skin on his side. He groaned his complaint, but he didn't try to rush her. Pleased, she gave him what he wanted. Her lips locked onto the hard puckered flesh, and she sucked him there. His body tensed, his head rolled side to side as he moaned, and when she flicked her tongue she felt his erection thicken in her hand.

She wasn't sure how he could control himself like this. Larry would have stopped her long ago, after a kiss or two, and by this time he would have been inside her, thrusting away with only vague concern for her pleasure.

David wasn't Larry. He wasn't like any other man she'd known, although she still couldn't identify what it was that had brought her here, to this most intimate of moments, with someone she barely knew.

What she was sure about was that she wanted to know him. More than his taste, or the sound of his pleasure.

She stilled her movements as she realized what she was thinking. The whole point of this exercise was to keep her distance. To focus on pleasure, on intensity, on anonymity. Yet the kind of knowing she was after had little to do with any of those things.

She wanted to know David. The person. How he thought, what made him laugh, how he viewed the world.

She straightened, and David stared at her.

"Susan? Is everything all right?"

She nodded, not sure what to say. If she told him the truth, it would spoil the plan. He wanted the same thing she did—anonymous sex, uninhibited hedonism. No. She wouldn't tell him. It was probably a passing thought anyway. She was just being sentimental.

She knew what she wanted out of tonight. His touch, his taste, yes. And familiarity. Until she felt comfortable with his body, until she could read him, she couldn't bring him inside her.

He'd be disappointed, but he'd live. Hell, he wouldn't even notice after she got through with him. She could do this.

"Hey?" David's whisper broke into her reverie and she realized she'd been staring at him without seeing him for a long while.

She smiled in anticipation. He was going to love her for this. "It's all right," she said, as she moved down the bed. "All you have to do is lie down. Let me do all the work."

"Wait a minute—"

She put her hand on his chest, stopping him from sitting up. "This isn't for you. It's for me. That you're going to like it is a bonus, okay?"

He shook his head, doubting her. He wouldn't for long.

She got to her knees, then climbed between his legs. Freedom of motion was paramount. Her gaze went to his straining erection, and for a long moment, she simply studied it. Somewhere between seven and eight inches and nicely thick, it was a beautiful specimen, veined and dark with a well-defined corona.

She touched him again, running one nail from the base of his penis to the head, on the underside vein. His muscles stiffened more, and when she glanced up, his eyes were closed, jaw muscle flexed.

Using the same path, she traced the line again, this time with the tip of her tongue. He quivered beneath her, especially where the shaft and head met. She tapped her tongue against that spot, not stopping until he thrust his hips up. Then, she took him in her mouth, but she didn't tighten her lips. Instead, she moved her head in a circular motion, causing his penis to slide to different places in her mouth.

His hissed, "Yesssssss," told her she was on the right track. Careful not to touch him with her teeth, she kept circling, circling, savoring his musky scent, the slightly salty taste of his flesh. She wrapped her hand around the shaft, as she tightened her lips a bit, then flicked her tongue as rapidly as she could.

He wasn't going to hold out much longer. In fact, if she read him right, he was seconds away from his climax. She placed her thumb at the very base of his penis, putting pressure on the vein. While she pressed, she began to suck, hard.

As it turned out, she didn't have to wait long. He groaned her name as he clutched the sheets in his fists. Releasing her thumb, she sucked as hard as she could, and that was it. He cried out, and she lifted her head, watching as his essence flowed, her hand still moving up and down his shaft.

He came for a long time in thick ribbons, and when he finally stopped, the rest of his body trembled.

The sight had aroused her more than she would admit. Something about his abandon, about the singularly male response made her feel incredibly female.

While he still had his eyes closed, she slipped off the bed and into the bathroom. After washing her hands, she dampened a hand towel with warm water, and brought it back to the bedroom. He hadn't moved an inch. Except, of course, for his chest rising and falling as he fought for equilibrium.

He jerked as the washcloth touched him, but then he sighed. When she finished, she tossed the cloth aside, then climbed into bed with him, snuggling close.

He wrapped her in his arms, bringing her close. He felt good, solid, warm. "Oh, my God," he whispered. "That was..."

"Yeah."

"I've never..."

"Ah, you're just saying that."

He chuckled and she felt the vibration in her cheek. "Something you should know about me," he said. "I don't lie. And I rarely exaggerate."

"Honest?"

"Very funny."

She ran her fingers over his chest, then twirled the fine hair. "David?"

"Yes?"

"What's your favorite color?"

He lifted his head, although she only felt it. Nestled in the crook of his shoulder, she couldn't see his face, which wasn't a bad thing. "My favorite color?"

She nodded.

"I don't know."

"Well, if you did know, what would it be?"

Again, she felt his laughter, the sound dark and rich. "Purple."

"Really? That's my favorite, too."

"I would have thought you were more red than purple."

"Sometimes. But mostly, it's purple."

"So I can stay?"

"What?"

"Because I like the right color?"

"It wasn't a pass/fail exam."

"What was it then?" he asked, his voice soft, and not really teasing any more.

She sighed, stalling for time. What should she tell him? That a part of her was balking at the setup? That she was intensely curious about him? That she thought she would be braver than this?

"Was tonight what you wanted?" he asked.

She lifted up on her elbow, needing to see his face. "Why?"

"You told me this was different. That you'd never done anything like it before."

"I haven't."

"Well?"

"It was great," she said, assured by the caring look in his eyes.

"But?"

She inhaled, then let it out slowly, prepared to jump into the deep end of the pool. This was different. And it could continue to be, if she let it. If she didn't chicken out. "I found myself wanting more."

His face brightened. "More?"

"Oh. Sorry. Not that kind of more."

He didn't pout. Big points in his favor. "Tell me."

She lay down again, snuggling as close to him as she could get. "More about you. Not just your body."

"Hmm. Is that a compliment, or did I do something terribly wrong?"

It was her turn to laugh. "No. You did everything right. Too right."

"How can something be too right?"

"When it upsets the game plan."

He was silent for a long while, but his hand on her arm started a slow, steady caress. Warm fingers rubbing her softly, sparking a low banked fire deep inside, close to the heart. "I'll tell you anything," he said.

"I believe you."

"Ask away."

"That's not it. I believe you would tell me anything, which makes it all right not to ask."

His hand stilled, but only for a few seconds. "Okay."

"I mean, if I thought you were hiding something, I could never be this vulnerable with you."

"But you don't know me."

"Yes, I do. That's the strangest thing of all. The moment I saw you, I felt I knew you. As if I'd known you forever."

"Really?"

She nodded.

"That's odd."

"I know. It's not like me at all. I'm usually very cautious. And it takes forever for me to really know someone. I've had the same group of friends since college."

"I meant it was odd because I felt that way about you."

"No, you didn't."

He squeezed her arm. "I did. Remember what I said? I don't lie."

"Did you feel that way in the scarf store? Or last Wednesday?"

"A little at the store. A lot last week."

"Maybe that's your libido talking."

"I've had many a conversation with my libido, and trust me, this wasn't one of them. This was a... I don't know. A feeling of familiarity. Of safety."

"Yes. That's it. That's exactly it. Only..."

"Go on."

"I didn't expect to want more."

"Ah, we're back to more."

"And I don't know what to do about it. I need to think."

He moved, dislodging her hand and her head, but he saved the situation by pulling her up so they shared the same pillow. He kissed her lightly, then held her gaze. "Why don't you do just that. Think it through. I won't lie and tell you it will be okay with me if you decide you don't want to see me again. But I'm negotiable. If you want to go the traditional route, all you have to do is say the word."

She studied him, looking for lies. Looking for that tiny spark of dishonesty that she'd never found in Larry. That was the problem. In all the years, with all the closeness she'd had with her ex, she'd never once suspected his true motives. So how could she trust this stranger? Despite his kind eyes, he was an unknown.

The one part of her plan she wasn't willing to abandon was that this time, she would lead with her head, not her heart. Fantasy, not fairy tale. "I'll let you know next Wednesday," she said.

"Same place, same time?"

"Exactly. Oh, and David?"

"Yes?"

"You have a choice here, too. I want you to think about this. If it's what you want."

"I don't need to." He leaned over and captured her lips for a bone-melting kiss. When he finally came up for air, he smiled. "I'm in," he said. "Whatever the game plan."

She wasn't surprised. It was sex, after all. With no strings attached.

He touched her cheek with his palm. "I mean that. Even if the game plan is to become platonic friends. Got it?"

She closed her eyes and let herself relax against his touch. She got it. She only hoped it was true.

8

IT WAS LATE, almost two, but David couldn't go to bed yet. Not with his mind racing like this.

The night hadn't turned out as he'd expected. In some ways, his imagination had been woefully inadequate. On the other hand, they'd parted company a bit too soon for his taste.

He'd wanted her. More than her incredible mouth. He'd wanted to be inside her. But he also realized this was new for both of them, that it was an experiment, really, where the outcome wasn't predictable. Of course that was one of the things that was so appealing about it.

Although he hadn't been thrilled when she'd gotten up to get dressed, he was glad she was able to tell him the truth about how she felt. Without rigorous honesty, it would all fall apart. Which meant he needed to be honest about his feelings, too. Only problem with that was, he wasn't sure what his feelings were.

Of course he liked the sex. Who wouldn't? The woman was incredible, and the fantasy aspect was something out of Penthouse Forum. But there was more here than just doing the horizontal bop. Susan had something to hide, and while he wanted to ignore that, it wasn't prudent.

Why wouldn't she tell him her last name? He'd gone over that question a hundred times in the last week. Was she married? If so, it was probably to someone prominent. But he hadn't seen a ring. Of course with her pale skin, she might have taken the thing off moments before he arrived.

If her marital status wasn't the issue, then what?

He shifted in his leather recliner, and felt the remote control under his left leg. The TV had been on for hours, but he hadn't noticed the program. It was a commercial, one that ran for a half hour of paid broadcast time, and this one was for cookware. He flicked the set off, and got to his feet. If he got to sleep in the next half hour, he could grab four hours. It wasn't enough, but better than nothing.

As he made his way to the kitchen for some water, he thought about bringing Susan here. He'd like to cook for her. Not that he was a gourmet, but he had a penne pasta dish that all his friends seemed to like, and even he could put together a salad. But Susan wasn't going to come here. She wasn't going to be part of his real life at all. Just in the shadows.

Maybe she was on the lam? While the notion had a certain romance to it, he had his doubts. So what else would make a woman as sophisticated and beautiful as Susan want to hide?

It was too much of a mystery for this early in the morning. He got his water, turned off the lights, checked the lock on the door, and headed for the bedroom. When he saw the bed, he pictured her, naked, lying on the sheets as she'd done those few hours ago.

The sense of longing hit him hard, along with a much baser want. He'd always liked puzzles, and for the life of him he couldn't imagine a more intriguing puzzle than Susan with no last name.

SHE WAS SCREWED. It didn't matter how she looked at it, how she rationalized her behavior, the truth was she was in it up to her eyebrows and she'd only seen him twice.

Susan sipped her coffee as she waited for Barbra to show up. Susan worked two to three days a week for the End Hunger Network, mostly on fund-raising. She didn't get involved with the big events like the telethon or the ad campaigns. Her expertise was in lobbying, and not just with politicians. She knew many rich and powerful people through her family connections and she wasn't the least bit shy about pressing them all for donations. They had it. She wanted it. It was a good cause.

She'd met Streisand on several occasions before, including one dinner at the White House. They'd never met one-on-one, however, and while Susan knew she should be nervous, come on, it was Barbra Streisand, she was too preoccupied with her Wednesday night dilemma to be intimidated.

Two days had gone by, and she hadn't stopped thinking about David. About what had happened between them. Lee had called her about a dozen times, worried sick about Susan's reticence to talk. Maybe that was a mistake, too.

She sipped her wine, checked her watch. The restaurant had been apprised of her guest, and they'd gone to great pains to make sure there would be no unwelcome interruptions. In fact, she was seated in a private room, that also acted as part of the wine cellar. The walls were red brick, with elegant hunting prints here and there. A fire crackled from an open hearth, and soft baroque music lilted gently behind the scenes. Altogether a warm, inviting ambiance. Perfect for her purpose. Barbra wasn't just going to give her money. She was going to give time and energy, which was the more precious commodity. Of course, the diva didn't know that yet, but Susan wasn't worried. She was very good at what she did.

A stunning young man came to refill her wine glass. In his early twenties, but evidently he had enough on the ball to be assigned to this room. Maybe it was just his looks—he was simply gorgeous with his dark hair, heavy-lidded brown eyes and a smile that could stop your heart. She looked at his name and smiled. "What does J.J. stand for?"

He lowered his lashes and blushed in an utterly endearing fashion. "Johnathan James, ma'am."

"Thank you, Johnathan James. Please give the sommelier my compliments."

He bowed with practiced ease. "I will ma'am. Thank you."

Ma'am. She hated when they called her that. She was only twenty-seven, for heaven's sake. Not a ma'am. But age wasn't the only arbiter of sobriquets. Money was quite sufficient. If you had enough, you were accorded every courtesy, whether you wanted it or not.

Money changed everything. And she had no doubt that her affair with David was no exception. She hadn't gotten to be a *ma'am* without learning something.

However, that wasn't her biggest concern at the moment. She had a lot of thinking to do that had nothing to do with David. She'd surprised the hell out of herself the other night. Her cynical heart had been shaken, and badly. She could have understood it if she'd known David for awhile. And even then, she would have thought her fear would have short-circuited any truly romantic notions.

Not that she thought she'd never marry. She would, she felt sure. But it wouldn't be with a stranger she met in a scarf store. She would end up with someone so similar to herself, they could have been pressed from the same cask. Which made sense. Like attracts like, and only someone in her circumstance could truly understand that.

It would help if she'd had even a sliver of interest in the men in her circle. Baxter Finch proposed on a regular basis, but he had a screeching voice that made her want to chew her own arm off. Dennis Forrester was another likely candidate whom she'd used several times as a convenient escort. Unfortunately, he had the personality of a wet dishrag.

Oh, it was foolish to go on about this. Her arrangement with David had nothing to do with social standings, marriages of convenience or otherwise, or prudence. That was the point. It was supposed to be all about wild abandon. About being naked, and not just physically. So why had she been so unhappy after she'd left the hotel?

Maybe unhappy was too strong. She'd loved being with David, and she wanted to be with him again and again. Only, she wasn't supposed to have felt anything except sexual bliss. Certainly not the ennui that had ensured a sleepless night.

She'd given herself a stern talking-to the next morning, right after coffee. She could have just what she wanted, as long as she kept her head. No sentimentality. No wishful thinking or schoolgirl crushes. Nothing but hot, unadulterated sex, and plenty of it. The kind of sex that made working out at the gym superfluous. Selfish, focused, anonymous sex. Why not? *Why not?*

A thought skittered close to the surface, one that sent a chill down her spine, but then there was a great clatter just outside the door, and she put David and her foolishness on the back burner.

She stood and smiled as her lunch date approached the table.

LEE TEMPLETON PICKED UP yet another baby magazine from the messy pile on the waiting room table. *Parents, Parenting, Fit Pregnancy, Child, American Baby, Mother and Baby.* Reading them all would be a full-time job, which at the moment wasn't such a bad idea, seeing as how she'd taken a leave of absence from her brokerage firm. Reading a magazine was about the only thing she felt like doing, except for sleeping and the ever-present eating.

"Can you believe all this stuff?"

Lee turned to the woman beside her, a pretty blonde who was as rotund as herself. "I know. As if it's not scary enough, now I feel like I'll miss the one article that will prevent me from raising a psycho killer or something."

The woman laughed. She seemed young, although when Lee looked into her blue eyes, she saw something more. Oddly, the word that came to mind was wisdom, but that was probably her hormones talking.

"Jane Warren," she said, holding out her hand.

"Lee Templeton." The handshake was warm and friendly, and Lee sighed. Maybe she wouldn't have to read after all. Although the doctor was the best OB/GYN in New York, she was notoriously tardy about appointments.

"When are you due?" Jane asked.

"Next month. Twenty-eight days to be exact."

"Are you kidding me? That's my due date, too."

"Well, how do you like that." Lee waddled back to her chair and maneuvered herself down. "Remember sitting down? Not planning to sit down, arranging yourself so you can sit down, then lowering yourself into a chair?"

"Yeah. And how about sleeping on your stomach. Remember that?"

Lee sighed. "I just keep telling myself it'll be over soon."

"Right. Then sleeping in any position will feel like a blessing."

Lee's cell phone rang, the current ring tone a snippet from Beethoven's Fifth. She dug into her purse, smiled an "excuse me" to Jane and hit the answer button. "Hello."

"It's me."

Lee snapped to attention. Well, maybe she didn't snap, but she did stop fidgeting. "Where have you been, Susan? Are you all right?"

"I'm fine. Just busy."

"Too busy for a phone call?"

"What do you think this is?"

"Ha ha. Now, tell me what's going on."

"Nothing. Oh. I had lunch with Barbra Streisand."

Lee shook her head, used to her friend's illustrious associations. "How's the marriage?"

"She glowed."

"I'll bet. Now, let's talk about something more important. What is all this crap about you canceling for Wednesday night? We've had that dinner planned for weeks."

"I'm sorry. Something has come up."

"Something? That's it? No more information? *Just something?*"

Susan's sigh made Lee even more concerned. It had been a long while since Susan had been really depressed. Please, God, it wasn't back.

"It's no big deal. Just some meetings I have to go to."

"On Wednesday nights. Right."

"Lee, it's nothing. I'm fine. I'm peachy. Can we change the subject?"

That made Lee blink. Susan wasn't like that with her. Ever. "Okay," she said, not wanting to press. "What do you want to talk about?"

"You. The baby. The weather. Oil prices. I don't care. Just not me."

"Honey, are you busy tomorrow? Can we do dinner?"

After a too-long hesitation, Susan said, "Okay."

"How about the Thai place on Park?"

"Seven-thirty?"

"Yep."

"Sorry for being such a bitch. I'm just tired. You take care and kiss Trevor for me."

"Will do." Lee cut the connection, but she didn't put the phone away. Not yet. The debate centered on calling the rest of the gang. Katy, in particular.

"A friend in trouble?"

Lee turned to Jane. "I'm not sure. Something's just off, you know?"

The blonde nodded, making her curls shimmer. "I do. I have a really good friend who's acting weird, too. Don't know why. Can't even tell you what's weird, exactly. But I'm absolutely sure something's not kosher."

"That's it. That's what's got me worried. Susan never kept secrets before."

"Are you sure?"

"Yes. No. I don't think so."

"Could it be a man? Someone she doesn't think you'd approve of?"

"I'm leaning that way. What about your friend?"

"It might be a woman. God, I hope it's a woman. David's the most wonderful man on earth, besides my husband, and it kills me that he's still single."

Lee raised her brow. "How old would this wonderful man be?"

"Thirty-two. And he's a psychiatrist. Not a creepy one, either. He's funny and smart and handsome, and women want him in droves, but he's looking for magic. Which seems to be in short supply."

"My friend is twenty-seven, gorgeous, richer than Chase Manhattan, and she's incredibly wonderful, too."

Jane grinned. "This has all the earmarks of a story with a happy ending."

"From your lips." Lee scooted forward, as much as she could, at least. "So, how do we go about getting these two wonderful people together?"

SUSAN WOKE EARLY Wednesday morning. The week had gone by in a blur of trying not to think about David while she thought about David. Not an iota closer to understanding what she wanted from him, or herself, or their arrangement, she was only sure of one thing: she was going to meet him tonight.

This time would be different, though. She wasn't going to try to plan their time together. In fact, she was going to let him lead the way. It would give her more insight into the man, and perhaps even make some things clearer for her.

She threw back her comforter and climbed out of bed. Wednesday had also turned into beauty day, which was actually pretty cool. She loved facials, although she was pretty impatient with the whole nail thing. Not the actual manicure—that wasn't bad. It was the drying portion that made her nuts. At least she had something to occupy her mind. Oh, boy, did she.

As she turned on the water for her shower, she thought about a comment Katy had made last night. The whole group had gone to Union Pacific for dinner. They eyed her suspiciously, asked pointed questions, which she'd ducked. Which bothered her. Katy had asked if she was in trouble. She'd said no, but she wasn't sure that was the truth.

Why she couldn't tell them about David confused her. It wasn't as if he was a Hells Angel biker or a wanted felon. He was a perfectly decent man whom she felt sure they'd all like. Only, they'd most likely want to know his last name. What he did for a living. All that normal stuff.

On her way home last night, she'd pondered telling them everything. Surely, they'd understand. They loved her. And they all understood her history. They'd been there when Larry and she had first met. Through the courtship and the wedding. They'd also been there for the breakup, and without her friends she would have gone out of her mind.

So what was she hiding for?

She stripped off her nightgown and stepped under the hot water. For a few luxurious moments, she didn't think of anything at all. But the doubts, so many of them, crept back in until she was quite sure she was certifiable.

David showed every indication that he was a good guy. A nice guy. She had no reason to doubt him, or her perceptions of him. Except... She'd thought the very same thing about Larry. And the others.

She had some kind of radar that honed in on lousy men. Put her in a room of a hundred guys, and she'd find the biggest bastard there, and fall instantly in lust, if not love. How many times did she have to get kicked in the heart to realize she wasn't very clever when it came to this whole man/woman thing? She might be cynical, but she wasn't made of stone, either.

She'd been hurt. Devastated by Larry. And the others since Larry had reopened the wound.

This was her time to heal. To protect herself. Of course, she could have continued being celibate, but frankly, that sucked. No. This thing, whatever it was, with David was perfect. No details. No entanglements. No falling in love. No pain.

And yet, she also understood that what she had with David was by nature intimate. And that she had a tendency to confuse sex with love. The syndrome was common for women, according to the self-help books she'd read. She'd done a lot of thinking about that. In truth, it wasn't the sex part that confused her. It was the before and after. The cuddling. The closeness.

So the best thing for her to do tonight was avoid all that. Get down to business, get off, and get out. Simple. A no-frills approach to sex in the city.

David might not be crazy about it, but there was no way he was going to end things because she didn't cuddle. He was a man, after all.

She focused on washing, and when she lathered her hair she found herself thinking of David, but her thoughts were anything but analytical. She pictured him with her in the shower, his hands instead of her own in her hair. Him pushing her against the wall, taking her hard as the water sprayed them both.

Shower sex. Yum.

With David, she could afford to take a risk. Physically, that is. She wasn't at all sure about an emotional risk. All she had to do was keep to the fantasies, focus on the sex. Keep her heart out of the picture.

God knows, the one thing that would screw everything up would be to fall in love with David. She simply couldn't go there. She wasn't that much of a masochist.

Get down to business, get off, and get out.

9

By TWELVE-FIFTEEN, David had completed the last step in his plan. He smiled as he left the Versailles hotel. She was going to love it. Talk about fantasies. Damn. He was getting hard just thinking about it. No. Thinking about *her*. Which was getting to be something of a problem.

He'd been a pretty typical teenager, horny as hell, inept and embarrassed. But he'd made the transition into young adulthood without many permanent scars. By the time he'd gone to medical school, he'd managed to take charge of his libido for the most part. His spontaneous erections were down to a minimum, and he'd felt reasonably in control.

Susan had shot all that to hell.

When it came to her, all bets were off. His body was in charge, and he had very little say in the matter. The world had narrowed to two states—*Wednesday* and *Not Wednesday*. The only surefire escape from his thoughts about Susan was work. When he was with a client, he focused. He wasn't about to let his personal life intrude when it came to his patients. They deserved all he had to give.

So did Susan, and tonight he was going to show

her that he wasn't all hat and no cowboy. It was his turn to direct the show, and he was leaving nothing to chance.

The doorman blew his whistle, hailing a taxi. A moment later a yellow cab pulled up. After tipping the doorman, David slid into the back seat of the warm automobile, and let his thoughts wander to his favorite subject.

What would she wear tonight? If he'd known how to reach her, he would have made some very specific requests. A dress, naturally. Those death-defying heels, and of course the garter belt and stockings. He also wanted her to wear a bra with a front closure, but he felt sure if she wore another kind, he'd be able to work with it.

Hell, it wouldn't be on her long enough to be a problem.

"We gonna just go in circles, man, or did you have a destination in mind?"

David snapped back to the present, and gave the driver his office address. His cheeks took a moment or two to cool off, but then he decided it was no big deal. The cabbie would get his money, whether they parked or drove. He had a half hour until his next appointment. So he settled back on the cracked leather seat and stared blindly out the window.

The real dilemma about tonight wasn't Susan's clothing. In his obsessive, constant preoccupation with her, he'd found himself yearning, aching to know her secrets. Her last name, to start with. But more than that, he wanted to know why she'd instigated this tryst. Why she'd selected him. What she wanted out of it.

Oh, screw it. He wanted to know everything about her, from how she liked her coffee to her thoughts on life after death. She fascinated him. Mesmerized him. Made him so hard he could poke a hole through a concrete slab.

The closer he got to his office, the stronger the urge became to tell the driver to keep on going. He didn't want to work. He didn't want to put Susan aside for anything. Jeez, maybe he's the one who needed a psychiatrist.

They turned on Lexington, right into a massive traffic jam. The cab jerked to a halt, the air filled with the cabby's inventive curses.

It wasn't far to his office, so David paid the man, gave him a generous tip, and left the warmth of the taxi for the bitter cold of the January afternoon. The smell of the city changed when it was this cold. Mostly, it was pleasant. The scent of snow, of wind. But living in Manhattan had taught him to expect a dose of bad for every good, and sure enough, when he got to the next block his senses were assailed by the sharp odor of garbage left out too long.

He hurried, unable to think properly under the influence of the stench. Thoughts of Susan had to be accompanied by good smells. A hint of flowers. An undertone of musk. The tang of spices.

Suddenly, her smell came to him, filled him, made him stop so sharply the woman in back of him nearly knocked him off his feet. He offered her a distracted apology, and went immediately back to the scent. It was still there. Not strong, but completely identifiable.

Had he conjured this magical odor? Or…

He looked around frantically, certain he'd find Susan by the storefront, next to the newspaper stand.

She wasn't there. Of course not. He'd imagined the scent, brought it forth by wishing, by remembering. He'd heard of such things, but he'd never experienced it before.

He wanted her this much. Enough to block out the whole city, the whole world. He wanted her to be part of him, to envelop him.

Tonight. He'd see her tonight.

HE MADE IT TO THE OFFICE a full seven minutes before Jack Gordon was due to arrive. Gordon wasn't a client, yet. He'd made an appointment to talk. Which was fine. David wasn't sure he wanted to tackle this one.

Gordon had just appeared on the cover of *People* magazine, voted Sexiest Man Alive for the unprecedented third time. His latest picture had grossed almost two hundred million domestically. He could write his own ticket, and that was something when first class in his business cost so dearly.

But that level of fame had a whole host of problems that came along with it. Ego, of course, but on a more mundane level, logistics could be something of a nightmare.

Phyllis had seen to the arrangements, of course, and if the press caught sight of Gordon, it wouldn't be because of poor planning. The last thing any of them wanted was for Gordon to be seen at a psychiatrist's office.

David poured himself some coffee and picked up a slew of messages from his in-box. As he settled at his desk, he flipped through the pink slips. Jane had called four times. Persistent little devil.

She wanted to set him up. Under normal circumstances, he would have agreed with no fuss. Jane knew his taste well enough. But at the moment, he had no room for another woman. Not even a nice woman, which she would surely be.

How could anyone compete with Susan? With the arrangement they had? He had no doubt that this thing with Susan wouldn't last forever, but while it did, he wasn't about to dilute his energy. The one thing he did need to do was come up with some kind of explanation for Jane. Something she wouldn't see through.

He'd have to think about that later. His buzzer sounded, letting him know Gordon had arrived.

SUSAN PUT HER PACKAGES in a row right by her bed. God, she'd made a pig of herself shopping. Anna Sui, Richard Tyler, Bottega Veneta, Fendi, and the two Kate Spade purses, just for starters. She wasn't even going to think about the shoes.

But at least her choices for tonight's wardrobe were more interesting.

The underwear portion had been taken care of three days ago, when she'd splurged on thigh-high nylons, tiny little G-string panties and a matching bra. She'd been rigorous about going to the gym all week. Nothing like the threat of a thong to make a gal work her ass off.

She pulled her clothes out of the bags and hung them one at a time, lingering over the Richard Tyler black velvet. Yes. Perfect with her pearls.

When everything was in its place, she made herself a cup of tea. With a couple of hours until she had to leave, she wanted to get calm. Let her adrenaline ebb. Even with all her misgivings and confusion, her upcoming date with David had kept her pumped the entire week.

She curled up on the chaise in the living room, sipped her tea and thought about the man. The way he looked at her. His expressive eyebrows. And his mouth. Good God, his mouth. When he kissed her…

So much for letting her adrenaline ebb. The very thought of him…

DAVID STUDIED HIS REFLECTION in the mirror. Nope. Jeans weren't going to cut it. Not tonight. Not for what he had in mind. He eyed his wardrobe carefully, and decided on the charcoal Armani with the silk Gaultier tie.

Off came the jeans, the T-shirt. As he put the discards away, he had to laugh. He'd never cared this much about what he wore. Not even when he should have. Not that he was a slob, but before this, he'd only considered appropriateness. Suits for work, tuxes for weddings, jeans for after hours. It was pretty simple. With Susan, all that changed.

He wanted her to like what she saw. Although his body was never going to win any awards, it didn't give him any trouble. He ran almost daily, swam three times a week, and played tennis whenever he found the time. He stayed in shape.

He changed his socks, then donned the suit. While he did his tie, he thought about his plan, and he nearly choked himself to death.

Could he pull it off? Would she laugh? Would she tremble? He voted for the latter. A few moans and a couple of gasps wouldn't hurt, either.

The woman wanted fantasy, he was going to give her fantasy. If he could keep his cool. Which was a very big if.

SUSAN GOT TO THE BAR just before eight, a bit winded from an unexpectedly delayed cab ride. She touched the back of her hair to make sure nothing had come loose from the black clip, then ran her hands down her dress. The velvet actually calmed her a bit. But that didn't last long.

As she sat on what was fast becoming her regular stool, the bartender approached with an envelope.

"For you, ma'am."

He wasn't coming. Dammit, she knew it was too good to last. He'd thought about it and decided to end it. Thanks, but no thanks.

"Ma'am?"

She took the envelope from the young man, not

Jay, and stared at it for several seconds. Maybe she didn't have to open it. Maybe she should leave, toss the note in the nearest trash can, and forget about it. Him.

With shaking fingers, she broke the seal and pulled out the linen paper inside. A room card key slipped into her hand, but she didn't let herself think what that could mean. After a couple of deep breaths to compose herself, she looked down.

Scheherazade, it began.

You are requested and required to appear before the king. He is in the mood for a story, among other things. He wishes you to follow his instructions exactly.

Go now to the ladies' room. Take off your panties. Put them in your coat pocket. Then go to the elevator and when you arrive at the suite, you *will* have hard, erect nipples. You will be prepared to please, or suffer the consequences.

Susan exhaled the breath she'd held forever. As she read the message again, heat pooled between her legs and in her breasts, and that unique tremor constricted her insides. His instructions weren't going to be difficult to follow—her nipples were already at attention. And as for the panties?

"Would you like a drink?"

She hadn't heard the bartender come back. She shook her head, pulled out a five to thank him for the note, then, on shaky legs, she headed for the ladies' room.

Inside the lush rest room, rich with overstuffed chairs, broad sinks with well-lit mirrors, fresh flowers, she went into the first stall. After hanging her purse on the hook, she lifted her dress, hooked her fingers in her panties, and pulled them down. Just as she was stepping out of them, the stall door next to hers opened. Susan's heel caught on the underwear, and she nearly lost her balance. Moving as quickly as she could, she straightened and shoved the small silk garment into her pocket.

Had the woman seen what she was doing? Just to be on the safe side, she waited until she heard the outer door close. Only then did she peek out, and finding she was alone, crept out of the stall.

No one would be able to tell about her lack of underwear, of course, and yet she felt exposed. As if her expression alone would give her secret away. She took a moment in front of the mirror to powder her nose, to refresh her lipstick. Every move sharpened her awareness of her seminaked state. Of course, that's why he'd asked her to do this. He'd known what it would be like.

She shivered again, anticipation making it difficult to focus on anything but her body and thoughts of the man on the fifteenth floor.

She left the rest room and walked to the elevator, keeping her gaze straight ahead. Even so, she saw a couple of businessmen giving her the eye as she passed. Ridiculously, her cheeks heated with a blush, and she walked faster.

Evidently, she'd been good in some past life, because she found herself alone in the elevator. As she rode up, she could feel her nipples hardening under her dress and bra.

At her floor, she gathered whatever wits she had left and headed for their suite. The card key shook as she slipped it in the lock.

David, stunning in a dark gray suit with a burgundy tie, his eyes aglow with seductive wickedness, stood just inside the room. He nodded at her, and she closed the door behind her.

"Come here," he said.

The whispered command compelled her forward. This was a new side of David, a more dangerous side. That she knew of his gentleness, his consideration, made her surrender easy. He wanted to play king for a night? Great. She'd play the slave girl for all she was worth.

He walked over to her, around her, studying her with an intensity that burned. She waited for his touch, but it never came. She felt his gaze instead. Felt his heat.

He stood in front of her again, nodded, his expression hard and purposeful. She almost reached out to him, let herself fall against him, but she stood her ground as the seconds ticked by in silence.

He walked away, and her breath caught. She willed him back, opened her mouth to call him. But she didn't speak. He went to the table by the couch, picked up a small glass and a bottle of Glenfiddich Vintage Reserve, pouring two fingers. His movements were slow and precise, designed, she suspected, to drive her crazy.

When he approached her again, he simply handed her the drink. She sipped it, the rare whiskey as smooth and hot as the man himself. She sipped again, twice, then handed the glass back to him. He found the slight lipstick stain on the glass and put his lips right there as he drank.

Then he went to the couch and sat down squarely in the middle. His gaze found hers, then led her to stand in front of him. After an excruciating moment, he leaned back. "Spread your legs," he said, in that same devastating whisper.

The words themselves were enough to make her bones melt, which made following his instructions more complicated. But she did spread her legs apart.

"Lift your dress."

Oh, God. Her stiff fingers curled around black velvet. Slowly, trying for the same precision she'd seen in his movements, she lifted the material, baring her thighs, the tops of her stockings. She heard his sharp intake of breath as the dress rose higher, revealing her naked flesh.

He focused on her sex, and she wondered if her sparse hair was enough to hide how wet she was. It didn't matter. He knew. Of course he knew.

"Turn around."

Keeping the dress at waist level, she did a slow turn, and when her back was to him, she stopped. It was difficult not to be self-conscious, knowing he was studying her rear end. But the self-consciousness was part of it. Him, in that suit, sitting on the couch. Watching her, pulling the strings, enveloping her in his fantasy.

She heard him shift a bit on the couch, and then there was music. Soft, seductive jazz. Familiar, but she couldn't place it. She swayed slightly as she felt the cool air of the room brush against her naked flesh.

"Bend forward."

She hardly heard the words, they were so softly spoken, but the message got through. It was almost more than she could stand. The flush in her cheeks set her face aflame, her fingers tightened on her dress as she struggled not to let go, not to run.

He didn't ask again, even though she waited long, long seconds, her heart pounding in her chest, her breaths labored and tight.

She closed her eyes.

Then she obeyed.

Slowly, slowly, she bent forward, keeping her back straight, her knees locked. She pictured what he saw, what she revealed as she moved lower still. Never had she felt more exposed. So naked. So incredibly turned on.

When her chest was parallel to the floor, she stopped. It felt totally wanton, completely shameless. She'd never been particularly modest, but this was outside her experience. Way outside.

He whispered something, and it took a minute for her to register the word. "Exquisite." He'd said it more to himself than her, and that prompted her to make her next move.

She arched her back, baring herself utterly to his gaze. Which made every nerve ending tingle with lust and need.

He groaned, a painful, longing sound that made her dizzy.

"So wet," he whispered. "For me. Tonight, you're mine. All mine."

She opened her eyes, wanting to turn, to be near him, not facing away.

As if he'd heard her wishes, he said, "Stand up."

She straightened slowly, not letting go of the grip on her dress.

"Face me."

With measured steps, she turned.

"Take off your dress."

The music—she remembered what it was. Gato Barbieri. The soundtrack to *Last Tango in Paris*. How appropriate. How sinful.

She lifted her dress little by little, inch by inch, until she reached her breasts. Then she paused, but not for long. Not when she could see the desire in his eyes, the tightness of his slacks.

When she pulled the dress over her head, she tossed it to him. He caught it one-handed, ran the soft velvet over his cheek.

Left in her bra, stockings and high heels, she felt like a courtesan, a geisha, a woman made for pleasures of the flesh. The music teased her, adding to the illusion.

"Pull your bra cups down."

His request made her bite her lower lip as she reached up to do as she was told. She'd worn the demi-bra, and even before she lowered the silky cup, a hint of her nipples was visible. And when she bared them fully, they tightened further, like two pencil erasers.

"Touch them," he said.

She moved her thumbs over the hard flesh, the sensations shooting through her, right down to her sex, making her muscles contract.

"It's time for your story," he said.

She'd forgotten. It was a wonder she'd remembered her own name, let alone a story. But it was his night. His fantasy. And she wouldn't let him down.

She closed her eyes as her fingers ran tiny circles around her nipples. Then she began her tale.

10

―――――――

"A LONG TIME AGO," she said, "there was a maiden who lived in a far-off kingdom. In this land, beauty was prized more than gold, and when this maiden, the daughter of a simple baker, was born, she was so perfect, so delicate, that everyone who saw her knew her destiny."

Susan ran her right hand down her body, skimming over her heated flesh, brushing the curls below. David's gaze went from her eyes to her hand then back again.

"In this kingdom," she continued," the most beautiful women were gifts to the king. So when she was of age, her parents packed her few belongings and took her to the palace gates. They were taken inside, and brought to the throne room.

"The king was very handsome. With fine brown hair, green eyes, a strong nose and jaw, he was as beautiful in his own way as the maiden. He bid her parents to say their final goodbyes, as this would be the last time they would see the maiden. She was his now, and she would live within the boundaries of the castle."

David's hand went to his zipper, lingered for a moment, then went back to his side. Susan could see the struggle on his face, and she decided to turn the screw even tighter. The music had changed, still jazz, but nothing she recognized. It didn't matter. It had a seductive beat, and she swayed in time. She ran her hands up and down her body, teasing herself along with him.

"The king dismissed his court so he could be alone with the maiden. She trembled in front of him, so afraid was she, that when he told her to undress, she didn't understand at first. He repeated himself, and this time, she caught the message and his impatience. Burning with embarrassment, the maiden took off her dress."

Susan reached behind her and unhooked her bra. She pulled it off and held it in her hand.

"As was the custom, she had no undergarments. The king held out his hand, and she gave him her dress."

Susan tossed her bra to David. It landed on his lap. He looked down as if he'd never seen a bra before. She had the distinct feeling that since all his blood had migrated south, his brain was a bit sluggish.

"The king ripped the garment into shreds, a gesture that told her everything about her future.

"He told the maiden that her body was his, her thoughts were to be only of him and his pleasure, and that she was to do everything she could to learn how to satisfy him with her body and with her mouth.

"And then, the king shifted forward on his throne, and the maiden gasped as she saw his thick, erect penis."

Susan waited a moment, and sure enough, David

shifted forward, too. She wondered if he was going to mimic the king, but he didn't. He just stared into her eyes.

"Without question, without pause, the maiden approached the king. And although she'd never done anything like it before, had never, in fact, seen a penis, especially one of such size, she went down on her knees before him—"

David startled her as he stood so abruptly he spilled the remains of his drink. "Enough," he said.

"My story doesn't please you?" she asked, knowing the answer.

"No," he said, the lie evident by the bulge in his slacks.

"Will this help?" she asked, as she brought her hands up to the clip in her hair. She released the clasp and shook her hair free, still swaying to the rhythm of the music.

"No," he said, his voice so gruff with desire it was almost a growl. "Go to the bedroom. Lie down."

She didn't argue. But she did brush him as she headed for the bedroom. Nothing. No reaction. His control made her shiver.

DAVID WATCHED HER WALK into the bedroom, sex on heels with her thick blond hair swaying across her back. He held rigidly still until she was out of his sight. Then he fell back on the couch and bit his knuckles to stop from whimpering pitifully.

Holy shit. It wasn't possible to be this turned on and not explode. He'd passed discomfort when she'd lifted her dress. From that moment on he'd been in real pain. Desperate pain. A stiff breeze could have made him come.

He had to calm down. He wasn't done. This was only the first part of the fantasy. The real thing was supposed to be next. Right. Like he'd be able to last another minute.

Baseball scores. That should work. Only he couldn't think of a single baseball team name. Okay. Time to get tough. He closed his eyes and thought of spiders. He didn't like spiders. Spiders, especially spiders inside his bathtub in the middle of the night, tended to make him scream like a girl.

As tarantulas inched along in his mind's eye, he could feel the pressure lessen where it needed to. Not much. Just enough to assure his survival.

He remembered the drink in his hand when his fingers started hurting. White from his bruising grip, he eased up on the tumbler and sipped the scotch. That helped, too.

Man, how long had he been out here? Susan was probably sleeping by now. Bored beyond belief. He had to get in there. Be masterful. Powerful.

He absolutely couldn't beg.

SUSAN SCRATCHED HER SIDE, then quickly brought her hand back up to the pillow. If he made her wait much longer, she'd have to come up with another pose. This one was making her stiff.

Diabolical. That's what he was. Staying out there, making her suffer like this. He was far better at this game than she'd dared hope. As the minutes dragged on, her thoughts had gone from titillating to shocking, and her whole body was on the edge.

She'd heard of women having orgasms without being touched. Unfortunately, she wasn't one of them. But she was close. Oh, so close.

She still couldn't believe how she'd bared herself to him. She closed her eyes, remembering the feeling of bending over, feeling the heat of his stare. Then seeing his state of arousal when she'd turned around. Powerful stuff.

Her stomach clenched again, and the urge to squeeze her legs together was nearly unbearable, but she forced herself to lay perfectly still.

She was rewarded with the sound of footfalls, and then he was at the door.

The way he looked at her was maybe the sexiest thing of all. His desire changed his whole face, made his eyelids heavy, his lips part, his breathing deepen. To be wanted so much was the surest aphrodisiac she knew.

He walked toward her, too slowly, but instead of joining her, he got the straight-backed chair from the small writing desk in the corner, and brought it to the foot of the bed. He sat down, sipped his drink. His gaze raked her from head to toe and back again. The muscle in his jaw flexed.

"Show me," he said.

She turned her head, not sure of his meaning.

"Touch yourself. Show me what you like."

Oh.

She'd never done this before.

''I'm not going to ask again,'' he said, in that low whisper.

The man was made of steel. How could he be so composed when she was so completely unnerved? She had to focus now. It was his fantasy, and he'd done so much for her already.

She ran her finger down her stomach, and as she reached her mons she closed her eyes.

''Open them.''

She obeyed. And was glad she did. He captured her gaze with his own, and his want, his need, seeped into her, and then she touched herself, skimming her outer lips, and whatever shyness she'd felt disappeared. He didn't look at her hands. Only her eyes.

She let instinct take over. Her fingers knew what to do, where to do it. Her legs spread farther apart, her left hand went to her nipple, she moaned with the pleasure, and still he kept his gaze on her eyes.

''Who are you?'' he asked, his voice so soft she barely heard him. ''How can I know? I want all of you. This pleasure, this intensity I have only with you. I can't stop thinking about you.''

The words shot a jolt of electricity down her spine that had nothing to do with sex and everything to do with sex. She gasped, wanting to stop, to listen, but she couldn't. Not when he looked at her that way. Not when he might speak again.

''I want you to know me, Susan. I want to be the man you see in your dreams. I want you to think of me every time you touch yourself. I want you to be mine.''

Her head jerked back and her muscles tightened.

She heard herself cry out as if from a distance, and then she was totally in her body, with her body, as she spasmed with the most powerful orgasm she'd ever experienced. She arched off the bed, squeezed her legs together even while her fingers continued to move, until the sensation was so extreme, she had to stop.

She gasped for breath, for equilibrium. And when she opened her eyes, David wasn't in the chair. He was standing next to the bed.

She rolled over and undid his belt with trembling, clumsy hands. Pulled down his zipper. She released his straining erection, already weeping in anticipation. She licked the wetness and just the light touch of her tongue made him groan.

She wanted him inside her. Desperately. But a small voice reminded her that tonight she was Scheherazade, and the slave girl always held something back. Always.

She took David's right hand in hers and wrapped it around his cock. He looked at her quizzically.

"Show me," she said.

He hesitated, but not for long. He stroked his length slowly, then curled his thumb over the head. She could tell he wouldn't last long; his chest rose and fell with alarming speed. He stroked himself again, and then he said her name.

She looked up. If she hadn't known better, she would have said he was in pain. He held onto her gaze as his jaw clenched, and then he came. She quickly put her hand underneath him. When he finished, she brought one damp finger to her mouth, tasted him as she got to her knees. Then she kissed him.

David pulled her into his arms, and lay down on the bed before he fell. His whole body trembled, and he couldn't get close enough to her. He kissed her hard and his tongue possessed her, never wanting to let her go.

But somehow, when she pulled back, he released his hold. It was probably for the best, as he was dizzy as hell. It wouldn't have surprised him if he'd passed out cold.

She smiled, touched the side of his face. "Next week is my turn. And I'm going to drive you crazy. I'm going to make you forget everything you've ever known."

He believed her. And it excited him. But not half as much as if she'd opened up. Told him what he wanted to hear.

When she kissed him again, he knew she was going to leave him. He wanted to change her mind, to convince her to stay. But he couldn't take another rejection. Not yet.

When she went into the other room, he closed his eyes. The next thing he knew, it was morning. And he was alone.

TREVOR KISSED HIS WIFE'S CHEEK as they waited for Susan to open her door. Something was going on with Susan, and although Trevor wasn't sure of all the details, Lee's concern was enough to make him nervous.

He loved Susan. They all did. And the last time she got all weird on them was during the really bad time with Larry. He hoped to hell she hadn't connected with that slimebag again, because Trevor would have to beat the crap out of him, and frankly, he was a lousy fighter. But he'd do it for Susan. He'd do most anything for his friends.

The door swung open slowly, and when Susan didn't look up, he tensed. So did Lee. He could feel it in her, though he only touched her shoulder.

"Come on in."

They entered her apartment, and as always, Trevor was impressed with the size and elegance of the place. Bigger than most homes, huge compared to typical Manhattan apartments, it was perfectly decorated, mostly in white. The furniture was all custom-built, except for the antiques. The paintings were large, and fascinating, and expensive as hell.

Susan led them to the couch. "Want something to drink?"

"Do you have any milk?" Lee asked.

"Yeah, sure. What about you, Trev?"

"I'd like something a little stronger."

"I've got some decent Chardonnay."

He nodded. When most people said the wine was decent, he had soda. But Susan knew her stuff. And the fact that he was a wine critic didn't intimidate her in the least.

She headed for the kitchen. He liked her in jeans, he decided. Especially when she was barefoot. With her hair in a ponytail, she reminded him of their college days. Things had been so simple then.

"See?" Lee whispered. "I told you."

"Okay. You're right. There's something wrong. But what are we supposed to do?"

"Talk to her."

"You start."

Lee sighed. "You're such a guy."

"Is that supposed to be an insult?"

"Only sometimes."

"Like now?"

She nodded. God, she was beautiful. It still amazed him that he'd gotten so lucky. His hand went to her stomach, to their child. Soon they would be three. It scared him stupid, but it was also so cool, there weren't enough adjectives.

Susan came back bearing drinks, and then she curled up on her leather club chair. "So, to what do I owe this honor?"

"We need to have a reason to come over?" Lee asked.

"No. Of course not. But you do."

Lee sighed. "Yeah."

"Go ahead. Shoot."

Lee sipped her milk, and when she took the glass away she had a tiny white mustache. "We're worried about you, Susan."

Susan grinned. "It's hard to feel threatened when you look like an ad for the dairy council."

Lee's hand went to her upper lip and she wiped it clean. "Don't change the subject."

"What subject is that?"

"You know what I'm talking about. You're being all secretive. And you don't call half as much. You've been spending inordinate amounts of time at the beauty shop, and despite your promise of just a few weeks ago, I happen to know for a fact that you've been buying shoes. Lots of shoes.''

Susan raised her brow. ''You have spies at shoe stores?''

''No. Merly Fisher saw you when she was shopping.''

''Why didn't she say something? I haven't seen Merly in months. How is she?''

''She's fine. She's gone back to brunette, and personally, I think it's much better than that strawberry blond. Her complexion isn't made for—''

''Hey.''

Lee stopped talking and they both looked at Trevor.

''Are we going to talk about Merly or what?''

Lee patted his arm. ''Sorry, honey.''

''Look, you guys,'' Susan said. ''Nothing's wrong, okay? I'm just going through a phase, that's all.''

''What kind of phase?'' he asked.

''I don't know. A phase.'' She got up and walked over to her Jackson Pollock, adjusting it a fraction and then a fraction more until she was satisfied.

Lee cleared her throat. ''Honey, are you seeing Larry again?''

Susan swung around, and from the look of horror on her face Trevor knew they didn't have to worry about that. ''Good God, no.''

''Please don't be mad at me,'' Lee said, grabbing his hand and squeezing hard. ''But are you seeing someone else then?''

Susan smiled wryly. ''No. I'm not. And I don't want to talk about this any more.''

"Okay. But there's just one more thing."

Susan looked at him for support. He shrugged.

"I have someone I want you to meet."

"Oh, no. No blind dates. You swore, Lee. You gave me your solemn oath."

"I know, but this is different."

"It's not. It's never different. So you can just forget about it. I'm not doing it."

"But he's nice."

"Lee, I love you like my sister, but don't push this. I'm not doing it."

Lee leaned back on the couch, her mouth curved in a pout that made him want to kiss her. He refrained, turning to Susan instead. "If you were in trouble, you'd tell us, right? You know we wouldn't judge you."

"Yes, you would. But then you'd accept me anyway. Which is why if I was in trouble, I would tell you. I'm fine. I swear it. I'm fine and I don't want you guys to worry." She looked at Lee's expansive stomach. "You have enough to think about."

Trevor studied his friend for a long moment, and while he still saw the shadow of a secret in her eyes, he knew they weren't going to get any more information out of her tonight.

"So," Lee said. "Are you going to just sit there, or are you going to show me the shoes?"

It was his turn to settle back. Shoes. He didn't get it. Women remained a great mystery, despite his status as a married man. He supposed that was a good thing.

Susan nodded with the most enthusiasm he'd seen in weeks, and headed for her bedroom.

When she was out of sight, Lee leaned toward him. "This isn't over," she whispered.

"I know."

"Okay then."

"Okay."

"Just act naturally."

He grinned. Lee cracked him up. Which was also a very good thing.

11

DAVID'S FATHER POURED schnapps into four shot glasses. Karen got hers first, then David's mother, and finally, he and his father lifted the pale liqueur.

"To family," Mel Levinson said, nodding with satisfaction at his brood. "May our tribe increase."

Karen sighed. The pressure to marry and have children was bad for both of them, but she got the sharp end of the stick. She was only twenty-four, but the way his parents went on, she was going to die an old maid. Were there old maids any more?

"Come to dinner," his mother said. "It'll get cold."

"Bea, it's salad," Mel said. "It's supposed to be cold."

"That's only the first course. I'm talking about the rest of the meal."

Mel shrugged in surrender, took Bea's hands in his and kissed her palms. "You're so gorgeous," he said, teasing her as he always had—as he always would, "I can't argue with you."

Bea pulled her hands away with a grunt, but David knew the ritual was as important to her as the sunrise. They would celebrate forty years of marriage in a few months. A lot of those years had been rough. Some had been incredible. By and large, the years had been full of love and laughter, and David figured that was the most a man could hope for.

"Hey," Karen whispered. "What's with you?"

"Nothing."

"Oh, please."

He looked at her, all in black, the uniform of the Manhattan yuppie, her red hair short and spiky, her eyes far too knowing. "I'll tell you later."

"I'm holding you to it."

He sighed as his father ushered them into the dining room. Of course his mother had set a perfect table, complete with candles, flowers, glasses of water and her mother's heirloom tablecloth. It was Friday night, and in this household, that meant his mother did the cooking instead of Ida, their live-in housekeeper. It was her time to connect with her children, to talk, eat, be together. He wished he could get here more often, but the harder he worked, the farther Pt. Washington, Long Island seemed.

He sat down in his usual place and looked at the family portraits on the wall. His grandparents on both sides had come from Lithuania during World War II. There were no pictures before that. But both families had thrived. His father was one of seven children, his mother one of ten. He had more nieces, nephews, cousins, aunts and uncles than anyone he knew. Most of them still lived in New York or New Jersey, and the holidays were always chaotic and expensive and pretty damn wonderful.

As his mother brought out the salad, he wondered what kind of neuroses he had that he was still single.

Was it that he felt he could never duplicate this? That he couldn't measure up to his father?

He hadn't questioned it much until Susan. But Susan made him question everything. From the ground up.

"So? Are you going to stare all night, or are you going to eat?"

He smiled at his mother. "I'll eat, I'll eat."

KAREN CAUGHT HIM just before he reached his car. "Not so fast, buddy boy."

"It's late. I'm tired."

"Tough. You're not leaving until I'm through with you."

David thought about arguing, but when it came to his baby sister, he always ended up giving in. Only, he was freezing, and he didn't want his folks to see them talking. "I'll meet you at Starbucks."

She nodded and headed toward her Jeep as he climbed into his BMW. He didn't get to drive it all that much in the city, but he loved the car, and when the weather was nice, there was nothing more relaxing than taking her out on the open road.

There was nothing open about the road he was on now. Three blocks from the residential street of his family home, he hit a strip mall, the scourge of modern man, and parked in front of the coffee house. Karen pulled up beside him.

There was no discussion until lattes were served, and they found a cozy corner to huddle in. Karen sipped her skinny hazelnut half-caf then nodded at him. "Shoot."

"You? My pleasure."

"Very amusing. I bet you wow all your dates with that rapier wit."

"That's not all. I'm humble, too."

She groaned. "Come on, David. Tell me what's going on. You've been really odd lately. Well, odder than normal."

"Thanks."

She didn't respond. The auburn brows rose, that's all.

"I'm seeing someone."

"No. Really?"

"You're such a wiseass."

"Just because I don't have the degree doesn't mean I'm not perceptive about human nature. Especially yours. So what's wrong with her?"

That stopped him. "What do you mean?"

"There's always something wrong with them. They don't read enough, they have too much baggage, they wear green on Tuesday."

"That's not true."

She cleared her throat.

"Shit. It is true. But, all those things are real."

"Uh-huh. Just like Aunt Esther's hypoglycemia."

He didn't rise to the bait. He was too busy running through a hasty checklist of past girlfriends. He'd broken up with every one, not the other way around. But, dammit, they did have legitimate issues.

"Okay, I didn't mean to send you into a tailspin. Just tell me about her."

"It's nothing."

"David."

"It's sex, okay? Just sex. Once a week. In a hotel. It's not going anywhere."

She didn't speak for a long while. She didn't even drink her coffee. She did study him intently, however. Finally, when he was just about to check for a pulse, she said, "And she's fine with this?"

"It was her idea."

"You do realize it can't last."

"Why not?"

"Women aren't built for such things. Perhaps if they're getting paid…"

"Karen."

"Just wondering. But I'm serious. Women don't do just sex. Maybe once or twice, but if it's ongoing, it's emotional."

"No, I don't think so. Mostly, I would agree, but with Susan—"

"Susan what?"

He coughed, nearly spilling his coffee. When he had his composure back, he shook his head. "I don't want to say."

"I know her?"

"Doubtful."

"Then what gives?"

Oh, crap. He wished they'd gone for drinks instead of caffeine. "I don't know her last name. And she doesn't know mine."

"Oh, my. This really is interesting. And how long has this been going on?"

"Five weeks."

"Cool."

"Why cool?"

"Because it's a mystery. She could be anyone. Or anything."

"So could I."

Karen grinned. "Honey, it wouldn't matter if you wore cowboy boots or a tutu, you'd still be David. Sweet, brilliant, quirky David."

"Quirky?"

"Edith Piaf. Need I say more?"

"But Susan doesn't know that."

"If she's seen you five times, she does."

"Am I that predictable?"

"Yeah."

"Gee, don't sugarcoat it or anything."

"I didn't say dull. You're not in the least. You're wonderful. Which is why all the single women you've ever met have wanted to marry you. Why married women you've met would be willing to leave their husbands."

What in hell? "Get out of here."

She shook her head. "You don't know, do you?"

"What?"

"That you're gorgeous. And pretty damn irresistible. Did I mention half the gay population wants you, too?"

"Karen. Knock it off."

She leaned over and kissed his cheek. "I suppose it's best that you don't know. It's so much of your charm. But listen to me, big brother—you're not built for this thing either."

"Meaning?"

"You want more. You need more. And if you'd

stop being so scared that you can't be the perfect husband, you'd be much, much happier.''

''You know what?''

''What?''

''You frighten the hell out of me.''

She grinned. ''I know. Because I'm gorgeous and brilliant, too.''

''I WANT YOU TO BE MINE.'' Susan replayed the words for about the five-hundredth time. It was Wednesday morning, and she had a zillion things to do. Not that her schedule had been enough to get her moving. It was almost noon, and she was still in bed. The problem boiled down to one simple fact: she was going quietly insane.

Men were possessive, she knew that. They wanted exclusivity, ownership. So David had simply been expressing that side of himself. It didn't *mean* anything. Certainly not the crazy things she'd been thinking.

He'd been aroused. Very aroused. People said things when they were that aroused.

If she told him the truth, the game would be over. The mystery would be solved, and then who the hell knows what would happen.

Better to keep things just as they were. Exciting. Erotic. Anonymous.

Or not.

She groaned as she tossed her comforter aside. If she had a brain in her head, she'd call her friends, confess all, and beg for help. Either that, or find a psychiatrist, pronto. No, somehow talking about it would spoil things, too.

But man, what if he was telling the—

Uh-uh. She couldn't afford to go there. She'd been wrong every single time she'd thought a man had truly loved her, and the risk was too great. She'd crossed an invisible line somewhere along the way, and the thought of losing David tore her up inside. Something told her, something deep inside her heart and her head, that while this relationship might not be the way she'd pictured happiness, it was as close as she was going to get.

She stood up, stretched and yawned. She had to get a move on if she was going to fulfill her promise. To make him forget everything. Drive him crazy. And her reward?

Tonight, she would feel him inside her.

DAVID WENT UP to the room, his heart beating its insane Susan rhythm, his cock already stirring. It was her night, and she'd made a promise. He could hardly breathe with anticipation. Only, she wasn't in the room.

She'd obviously been there. Glenfiddich scotch was on the coffee table along with two glasses and a vase of yellow roses. Her coat was on the chair, along with her purse. His gaze moved to the bedroom door. Closed. Okay, then. They were going to jump right in.

He took a few steps toward the room, then remembered his coat. Stripping it off, he tossed it vaguely on the couch, not caring in the least where it landed. He poured himself some whiskey, downed it in one gulp then coughed for a few moments. Once that was done, he wondered once more if he'd made a mistake coming in jeans instead of Armani.

He shook his head at this new level of idiocy. Who cared what he wore? They were going to be naked in a few minutes anyway. At least he prayed they were.

He ran a quick hand through his hair and this time he made it to the bedroom door. He pictured her a hundred ways, each more alluring than the last.

His imagination wasn't even in the ballpark.

Susan sat primly at the foot of the bed, her hands folded in her lap, her head bowed demurely. She reminded him of a schoolgirl in the principal's office. Except, of course, that Susan was naked.

Oh. And there were two neatly coiled piles of silk rope on either side of her. Not to mention the blindfold.

"Do you remember the fantasy I told you about that first night in the room?"

"In excruciating detail," he said, stunned that he could speak at all.

"Tonight, we're going to make it all come true."

To say he got hard would mock every other erection. The soundtrack of his blood rushing from his brain was disconcerting, but it didn't prevent him from taking a few more steps toward heaven.

She smiled at him, then turned her gaze toward the bathroom. He got the hint and looked there, too. A razor. Shaving cream.

He jumped when he felt her hands on his shoulders. He hadn't heard her stand. He had no idea how much time had lapsed. He was deeply into a fugue state, and he hoped fervently that he'd never wake up.

His focus went to the woman, and her delicate fingers opening button after button on his shirt. After each, she kissed the exposed flesh, her lips cool, her breath warm. And she didn't stop until she reached his belt. Then she pulled the shirt off, folded it neatly, and put it on the chair.

He reached for her, but she was too quick; she'd knelt before him and touched his shoe.

"David?"

He nodded.

"In order for the shoe to come off, you need to lift your foot."

He nodded again, and let her raise his foot. Off came the shoe and sock, followed by a repeat performance with his other foot.

His breath stopped as she rose, slowly, but she didn't stop until she was fully upright and her gaze had locked with his. He wanted to ask her about the pants. But he didn't. Because she took his hand and led him into the bathroom.

The walk jolted him out of his inertia, and he took over. First, he spread a towel on the counter. Then he kissed her lightly on the lips, teased her with his tongue. His hands moved to her waist and he lifted her onto the counter next to the sink.

God, she was so beautiful. He could see the curve of her back in the mirror, the delicate lines of her neck. He wanted to touch her everywhere, kiss, lick, suck, nibble his way up one side and down the other. But it was her fantasy, not his. "Wait right there," he said.

He dashed out, grabbed a pillow from the bed, then

went back to the bathroom. He put the pillow behind her, so she wouldn't get cold when she relaxed into position.

He ran his hands gently over her upper body, her neck, chest, breasts, drowning in the sea of her softness. When he reached the top of her thighs, he spread her legs.

He'd never shaved anyone else before. It posed some interesting logistical problems. But he hadn't been a Phi Beta Kappa for nothing.

He turned on the water, got a washcloth, and when it was the right temperature, he laid the terry cloth over the sparse blond hair.

She inhaled sharply.

"Too hot?"

"No. Fine. Just...intense."

"Right."

He put some shaving gel on his fingertips, then removed the cloth. Touching her was a completely new experience. The way she sat, open, vulnerable. The light in the room. His own reflection in the mirror. It was surreal and as erotic as anything he'd ever done before.

He used the razor carefully, grateful he wasn't shaking. He turned the water on and rinsed the safety blade often. As he moved lower, she shifted until she was almost at the edge of the counter, and cleverly, resting her feet on his shoulders.

Her sharp, rapid breaths hinted that she was enjoying herself, but it was her half-lidded eyes and slightly parted lips that made him sure. He had to force himself to pay attention to the job, and not get lost in her expression.

Finally, it was done. He ran his fingers over her puffy flesh. He'd never felt anything softer or more inviting. A second washcloth came into play as he wiped away all traces of gel. She moved her foot, but his hand on her ankle stopped her. ''Not yet,'' he said. ''I have to make sure I did a good job.''

Her smile lingered in his mind's eye as he knelt to the task. Pulling her even closer to the edge, he explored her with his lips, his tongue, tasting not a hint of shave gel. After he was satisfied that her outer lips were as smooth as a baby's bottom, he dipped inside her. Her taste made him tremble, her softness made him harder still. And when she moaned, grabbed hold of his hair, he nearly lost it.

It was time to focus. To hone in on the sweet spot. Her cries grew louder as he tongued her hard and fast.

She came with a violent spasm, knocking the shaving gel can to the floor, ripping out a nice chunk of his hair, and squeezing the life out of his neck with her feet.

It was fantastic.

After she'd come down from the ceiling a bit, he stood and pulled her into his arms. She melted against him as he carried her to the bed. Placing her carefully in the middle, he took each of her languid limbs and fastened them to the four corners of the bed. The silk ropes would do her no harm, even if she got very energetic. She moaned as he finished the last of her bonds. Only the blindfold remained, but before he put it on, he kissed her.

Her passion poured through him, and while he wanted to take his time, to prolong his pleasure and hers, he knew that wasn't gonna happen. He was painfully ready. Just the thought of being in her made it hard to think, to breathe.

Another kiss, and then he smiled. "I'm going to put the blindfold on now. If you want me to."

She nodded, closing her eyes in sweet surrender. He was careful to place the mask perfectly, to make sure no hair was caught, that there was no discomfort.

When he stood again, he let his gaze linger on the exquisite picture in front of him. Her breasts, nipples hard as pebbles, trembled with each breath. Her long limbs stretched out, made more beautiful by the ropes. And her sex, bare and impossibly naked, still pink and swollen from his ministrations.

He unbuttoned his jeans, and eased them and his shorts over his erection. Once he was clear of that obstacle, he let the pants drop, then kicked them aside.

Only one thing left to do. He went into the bathroom, drank a glass of water, then filled the glass again for her. He shut the light off with his elbow, and headed for the promised land.

His foot came down on something cold and hard, the glass flew out of his hand, and he was falling and then incredible pain and it all...went...black.

12

"DAVID?"

A surge of adrenaline shot through Susan, and she almost dislocated her shoulders trying to sit up. She struggled for a moment, gasping with frustration, as fear took over her world. Blind, immobilized, the mental pictures flashed through her mind like a slide show—David bleeding, David dying, David dead. She fought her bindings again only to give up with a whimper. Why had he been so damn thorough?

She scooted as far as she could to her right, then bent her head until her arm brushed the blindfold. For several eternal minutes, she struggled with the mask, almost losing it several times. When she finally succeeded in dislodging the stupid thing, the blindfold was wet with her tears. She raised herself as high as she could go, but all she could see of David were his bare feet.

"David. David. David!"

Nothing. Not even the slightest budge.

Oh, God. This was bad. This was so bad, she wanted to throw up. She wanted to scream.

Scream. Yes. If she screamed, someone would come. Someone would save him.

And find her tied to the bed, naked and shaved.

Oh, God.

She fell back on the pillow, willing herself not to panic. The last thing she needed now was a full-blown anxiety attack. There was a solution to this problem. If she could calm herself enough, she'd see it.

Only, what if David really was seriously hurt? Or worse? What would it matter, then, who found her and in what condition? His life was at stake—it was no time to worry about modesty. Or anonymity.

God, please…

A new, deeper wave of panic washed through her. He couldn't be dead. He couldn't be.

Oh, God, she'd been clueless. Blind, stupid. An idiot! She'd fallen for the guy while she'd been busy with her silly fantasies.

"David!"

Was that a moan? Yes. It was. Of course. He was okay. He'd come around in a minute. A concussion maybe, but that's all. He'd be fine. They'd go to the emergency room, and he'd make a joke about the bump on his head, and they'd laugh and everything would be normal.

Except that now she knew. What had started out as a game had morphed into something far more serious. She couldn't bear the thought of David gone. Wednesdays had become the center of her life. She thought about him all the time. She dreamt about him, woke up to the image of his smile. Her body reacted to him even when it was just a thought. Even when she overheard the name.

She moaned, her voice sounding unnaturally loud with so much silence around her. The thought spurred a surge of hope, and she closed her mouth tightly, holding her breath, listening as she'd never listened before. Was that him? Dammit, why couldn't she quiet her heart, the blood rushing through her veins. If only she could be quiet enough, she'd hear him breathing.

But she didn't.

She cared for David. Cared for him as she'd never cared for another soul. *Differently.* She craved his touch, his laugh, his crooked nose. She loved his deadpan expressions that he liked to think he was safe behind, and the way she could read him like a book. She loved his scent, his passion, the taste of his cock, the feel of his thighs. When she was with him, she felt safe.

The irony made her choke out a bitter laugh. Safe. That was the last thing in the world she was. Not just because she was tied up naked on a hotel room bed and that David was, *please God,* lying unconscious on the floor, but because the only reason she felt *safe* with David was because he didn't know who she was.

And she knew, as surely as she knew her last name, that once the truth came out, nothing would be the same. Not just on his part. On hers. The moment he knew, the walls would come up again. Every conversation would be examined for ulterior motives. Every nice thing he did for her would be suspect.

She didn't know another way. Damn it all to hell, doubt had become second nature to her. There were people she trusted implicitly: her family, Lee, Trevor, Katy, Ben, Peter. Not a very long list. And there was no one on that list who could possibly give her what David had.

The truth of it was, she wanted to love, and be loved in return. But love was faith. Love was respect. Love was trust.

Her plan had been a good one. Well thought-out, perfectly executed, but for one thing. David had awakened her heart. Damn him. Damn herself.

She sniffed, wiggled her nose, unable to do much else with her stupid hands tied. As she sighed and pulled at the ropes again, a noise stopped her. She froze, held her breath, listened. Was it...

She cried out with relief. Trembled as the adrenaline pulsed through her. Wept until she couldn't see. "David!"

He answered her with a groan.

"David, are you all right?"

"Uh, I think so. Shit."

"What? I can't see you. Are you bleeding. Call 911. No, wait, I have my doctor's home number in my purse. No, sorry, no, he's out of town. Call 911. Maybe there's a doctor here at the hotel—"

His laughter slipped through her blather, and it was the best news she'd had ever. If he was laughing, he had to be all right. He had to be whole. Safe. *Safe.*

Then she saw the top of his head, the brown silky hair disheveled and spiky, but the most welcome sight of her life. She winced as he revealed a lump the size of a robin's egg on his forehead. But the gaze that met hers was steady, if a little surprised. And his lips curled into a genuine, slightly embarrassed grin.

"I was so scared," she said.

"I'm sorry."

"It's not your fault. You slipped."

He looked behind him, then shook his head. "Shaving gel."

"Next time, maybe we should try waxing."

He laughed, winced, put his fingertips to the lump on his head, and laughed again. "I have to say, I'd do it again in a heartbeat if I got to wake up to you." He sat on the edge of the bed. "You're so incredible."

"David. You probably have a concussion. We need to go to a doctor."

"I'm fine." His hand went to her thigh and he touched her so lightly she got goose bumps.

"You're not. Come on. Stop. Untie me."

"Untie you? But we still have a whole fantasy to—"

"Hey," she said sharply. "It's not my fantasy to have you keel over from a brain aneurysm while we're doing it. That tends to dampen my libido for some reason."

He nodded and his grin faded. "I suppose you're right."

"So untie me, okay? Let me get dressed, and then let's go."

He turned to her right foot, and the rope tightened, then loosened, then was gone. He walked around the bed, and did the same to her left foot.

Susan watched him, glad he was still shirtless. Sorry the night had to end this way. More grateful than she could ever say that he was safe. That he was alive.

Scared spitless about how she felt.

The thought came again, this time with a new urgency. *Tell him. This time will be different. This time, nothing will change.*

He finished untying her and she brought her hands together, feeling the ache from her struggles. She massaged her wrists for a moment, then sat up, terribly aware of her nakedness. She wanted to dive under the covers, and that hadn't happened before. Instead, she slipped off the bed and went straight to the bathroom, closing the door behind her.

David lowered himself to the bed, his hand a hell of a lot shakier than he'd like to admit. He knew he'd been unconscious, but for how long? When he'd seen her raw wrists, it had been all he could to do keep it together.

Shit. What kind of moron knocks himself out when he's got the most beautiful woman in the world tied to his bed? If there were prizes for the worst luck, he'd be right up there with the captain of the Titanic.

He lowered his head and winced as blood pounded around his temple. He'd really done a job. His fingers told him he would hurt for several days, that he most likely was concussed, but it was nothing earth-shattering. Worse, far worse, was that she was probably too afraid to try this again. It was like getting the best bicycle in the world, and having it taken away after a spill. Totally unfair. Come on. What were the odds of anything like this happening again?

He sighed, and went off to gather his clothes. In slow motion, more from disappointment than weakness, he put on his shoes and socks, then his shirt.

His hand brushed his semi-erect cock and he silently apologized.

The bathroom door opened and he turned too quickly. Dizziness made him reach for the wall, but it was Susan who supported him, helped him sit on the bed. Her worried expression did something odd to his insides. Or was that the concussion? He wasn't sure. All he knew was now that he had her, he didn't want to let her go.

"Do you want some water?"

He shook his head.

"Can you walk?"

Nodded.

Her brow wrinkled. "Maybe I should call an ambulance."

"Nope. I'm okay. Dizzy. You're right, I think I do have a concussion, but I doubt it's serious. I remember the fall. That says a lot."

"What do you mean?"

"If I had suffered more than a superficial wound, I'd probably have amnesia."

"You're kidding."

"Nope. Not big time. Usually it's an hour or so preceding the incident. Sometimes a day."

Her expression changed to curiosity. "David, are you a doctor?"

He smiled. "Of a kind."

"Don't tell me you're a gynecologist."

He laughed. "Nope."

"What?"

He looked into her blue, blue eyes. "Are you sure you want to know?"

"The ship has sailed. I might as well know if it's a luxury liner or a tugboat."

"I'm a psychiatrist."

Her already pale face grew whiter still. In fact, she was the one who looked like she'd been knocked out. "Susan?"

"Huh?"

"What's wrong? I'm a psychiatrist, not a serial killer."

"You're a shrink, and you went along with this? With all of this?"

"I'm a man first."

"But—"

He reached over and took her cheeks between his hands, forced her to meet his gaze. "Nothing has changed. I'm the same man as I was five minutes ago."

"You probably think I'm a loon."

"No," he said, shaking his head solemnly. "I know you're a loon."

She pulled back, startled. "Thanks a lot."

"But a nice loon. A wonderful loon." He captured her face again, and before she could fly away, he leaned in for a kiss. "An incredible loon."

"Is that your idea of a compliment?" she whispered, her breath sneaking between his lips.

"Uh-huh."

"Smooth. Great bedside manner."

"Thanks."

"David, I'm not kidding here."

"Neither am I." He finally pulled back, away from those tantalizing lips. "I'm no saner. I'm as much a loon as anyone else. We're all eccentric and odd and confusing and contradictory. It's what makes us interesting.''

She studied him for a long moment. ''Interesting.''

''Yeah. Now, there are people who cross the line. Where eccentric becomes erratic, and the confusion doesn't end. But mostly, we're all just struggling to make sense of things, of our humanness.''

''A psychiatrist,'' she repeated, more to herself than him. ''I can't believe it.''

''A pretty damn good one.''

''Well, sure. I can see that.''

''But?''

''It's just that—''

He smiled as sincerely as he could, encouraging her to talk.

''I don't know. It doesn't matter.'' She stood so abruptly, he almost fell.

''It matters,'' he said, finding his equilibrium in more ways than one. ''Tell me.''

''I can't.''

Disappointment urged him to push her, but if she wasn't ready, then she wasn't ready. ''I understand,'' he said. ''The accident pushed the intimacy into a new level. And then I told you something about me, which had to be jarring. I see that it's important to you to keep your life to yourself, but I want you to know that nothing you could tell me would make me feel any differently.''

She looked away briefly, then back at him, her eyes changed yet again, this time with sparks of anger.

"Thank you, Doctor. Will you be leaving a bill for the session, or is this one gratis?"

Her reaction stunned him. He wasn't analyzing her, just making an observation. And then he got it. She needed distance. Time to think. "It's okay," he whispered as he approached her. His hand went to her cheek, but she ducked back, turned and left the bedroom entirely.

"Stupid," he whispered to himself, cursing further as he followed her. She'd misunderstood, and he wasn't sure how to explain.

She stood by the chair, lifting her coat, not looking up when he approached.

"Susan, wait."

"I'm going downstairs, and I'll get you a cab. I think there's an urgent care just a few blocks from here."

"Susan—"

She turned to him then. The anger was still there, but hidden behind a facade of steely indifference. "I'm sorry about what happened," she said. "I never wanted you to get hurt."

"I never wanted that for you, either."

"I'll be fine. I'm always fine." She grabbed her purse and headed for the door.

"Will I see you next Wednesday?" he asked, afraid his desperation would make her say no, but unable to hide it.

She put her hand on the door lock, but she didn't open it. Seconds ticked by slower than his heartbeat. If he could have, he'd take back everything he said.

Turn back time. He needed these nights. Needed this space, this woman. "Please," he whispered.

"I don't know." And with that, she unlocked the door, and left him with his bruises and his regret.

DAVID PICKED UP HIS PACE as he crossed 7th Avenue. He had this odd feeling, as if someone was watching him. Ridiculous, of course, but he couldn't shake it. He'd paused by store windows and stared unobtrusively at the people who passed, but no alarm bells went off, nothing out of the ordinary occurred.

Maybe he was just being paranoid from the gossip in today's *Post*. His client, Jack Gordon, was on page one, which would have been fine for the actor except that the article was one blatant innuendo after another, all pointing toward his sexual preference.

David didn't envy Gordon. Fame was a terrible taskmaster, and the price was often too heavy for mere mortals. To live in a world where it was always open season on one's life, one's privacy, would tax a saint. And most of the actors he knew weren't.

They never got used to it. He'd known too many really famous people to believe the hype that they brushed it all off, ignored the lies and the dirt. Despite their profession, despite the obscene amounts of money they made, they were, on the whole, still flesh and blood. Not made of stone.

The hairs at the back of his neck stirred, and he paused at another store window. This one a luggage shop. But he didn't look at the suitcases. His gaze was on the reflection of the people behind him.

There. That guy in the black trench coat. David

recognized him. And what the hell was that behind his back? A flash of silver scared the hell out of David and for a moment as it occurred to him it might be a gun.

Jesus. His clients weren't the only people in the spotlight. How many times had he seen his own name in the New York papers? Too often. His reputation had spread in the last few years, and with it, his presence in the tabloid society.

He stood stock-still, waiting for the man to make a move. The guy was big, well over six feet, and built like a refrigerator. His coat needed pressing, and frankly, so did his face. He'd picked up a magazine from the stand at the corner, and flipped the pages, but his gaze never went to the articles. He was following David. No doubt about it now. But what should he do? Confront him? Try to ditch him? Maybe jump in a cab?

A woman walked in front of the reporter, and David jolted. No, it wasn't Susan. Just a tall blonde with her hair pulled up in a clip.

And then it occurred to him that perhaps this reporter had nothing to do with Jack Gordon. What if this was about Susan? He'd never tried to be discreet going to the hotel. If her secret was as big as he guessed, it wouldn't be out of the question for them to have been followed.

His face infused with angry heat, his objectivity instantly gone. If that bastard tried to get to Susan—

David turned abruptly and in two seconds, faster than the man could react in anything but surprise, he was in the guy's face. "Who are you?"

"Hey, man. I'm just minding my own business." The man spoke loudly, clearly trying to gather an audience.

David grabbed his hand, and pulled it from behind his back. Sure enough, he held on to a camera. "Who are you after? Tell me, you bastard, or I'll hit you so hard you'll have a whole new face."

"You can't do that. There are laws."

"I know. And I have the best attorney money can buy. I'm willing to go for it. Are you?"

The guy pulled back, tried to loosen David's grip. When he realized there was no chance, he slumped. "You're Jack Gordon's shrink. I know. I've been watching."

"What the hell did you think you'd get? I'm a doctor, you idiot. Everything told to me is confidential."

"I'm not looking for a quote." He glanced at the camera. "Word is, the guy's a fag. If I can catch him in the act—"

David's fist came up, and it was only through inhuman effort that he didn't smash the guy inside out. He wanted to, though. Man did he. But there were consequences. Always there were consequences.

He lowered his hand, gratified at least to see the man was shaking. "I'm not a public figure. Ask your lawyers, they'll tell you. So if I see you again, I'm putting you behind bars so fast your head will spin. And I will prosecute you to the full extent of the law. Who knows. You might make a good living off of prison photos."

"Okay, okay. I'm just doing my job."

"Your job is despicable." He released the man's collar, pushing him backwards, into the side of the newsstand. "And so are you. Stay the hell away from me."

The photographer took three steps back, so he was out of arms' reach. "You think you can hide from us? Not a chance." Then he darted into the street, narrowly missing an oncoming car. The cacophony of horns followed him as he ran.

All the air seeped out of David's lungs. He was tired. Tired and unsettled, and all he could think about was Susan. Whether she would show up on Wednesday. Lately it felt like the only safe place he knew was in her arms.

13

SUSAN STARED at her laptop screen, mesmerized by the blinking cursor. She'd meant to do her e-mail, to check on a bid or two at eBay. Instead, she'd gone into her word processing program and started to write, ostensibly to figure out why she'd been so upset with David. That answer had come immediately—she'd been caught off guard. She'd gotten scared that he had seen too much. That he'd already figured out she was terrified of... Of what?

I don't know what I want, she'd written. *I can no longer pretend it's just sex. He's more than that, much more, but what?*

She read the few sentences for a third time, then started typing once more.

I think about him too much. Give him too many good qualities. Maybe I don't want to know him so that I can make him anything I want him to be. Maybe I don't want him to know me so I can make *me* anything I want to be. But now, the person I'm pretending to be is falling in love with the person I'm pretending he is and how screwed up is that?

Okay, so what do I really know?

He's as sexy as hell. He turns my knees to jelly the moment I see him. He's considerate—careful not to push me too far, or to assume anything. He listens. He's a psychiatrist!! He has a wonderful sense of humor. He's gentle, but when he takes charge it's one hundred percent dominant male, which turns me into a quivering puddle. He shows up when he says he's going to. He smells wonderful. He has the best chest in the northern hemisphere, and his ass should be on the cover of *Time* magazine. He makes love like a—

She paused. In fact, they hadn't made love. Not once. They'd had sex, but even that had been safe, careful. Erotic, yes, but it wasn't making love. Making love was about connection, about vulnerability, about surrender. What they'd done was about intensity, danger, risk. It was supposed to have been about anonymity and fantasy, but her biggest fantasy now had nothing to do with being tied up or role-playing. It was about love. Which scared the hell out of her.

Again she wrote the main question on her computer. *What do I want? If I could have anything, what would I want?*

Guarantees. Certainty that he would love her unconditionally, that her money, her family, her hang-ups, would make no difference at all. That he would love her forever, and never break her heart.

She chuckled, although her amusement had more to do with her own foolishness than her wishes. There were no guarantees in life. She had no reason to think

love was even an option for David. She remembered
a quote she'd read that had stuck with her: To risk
loving, knowing loss was inevitable, is our greatest
challenge. Yes. The only thing that was certain was
that loss was inevitable. Inevitable.

Given that, what did she want? Given who she was,
and who David was, and what life was, what was she
willing to risk?

She stared at the cursor, her fingers poised, but no
words came.

DAVID'S PULSE POUNDED as he walked across the hotel lobby. He willed her to be there, to be happy to
see him, to forget about what he'd said last time. Yes,
he wanted to know more about her, to know everything about her, but he wasn't going to blow what he
had. The need for her was so powerful, he dared not
risk scaring her off. So he wouldn't. He'd play nice.
He'd keep quiet. He'd be satisfied with whatever she
wanted to give him. Just please, let her be there.

He got to the bar doorway, hesitated for a few seconds, then walked in. She was sitting there, and he
breathed again.

God, she was so beautiful it changed him. Literally.
His body shifted, became something new, something
he couldn't be without her. And she hadn't even
turned around.

When she did, when he saw the smile on her face,
the eagerness in her eyes, the relief made him grin
like a fool.

She touched her hair as he walked toward her, wet-
ted her lower lip with the tip of her tongue. When he

leaned down to kiss her, he noted the flush on her cheeks, the quick intake of breath. The kiss was supposed to have been brief, a hello. But once his lips touched hers, he couldn't leave without tasting her, without breathing in the scent that flew him to the moon.

Finally, he pulled back, his desire to get up to their room taking precedence. Her blush had deepened, and he wondered if she'd been thinking the same thing he had—upstairs, they could be naked, while down here in the bar, people tended to frown on such things.

"Do you want a drink?" she asked.

He shook his head. "I only want one thing."

She stood, called over the bartender to take care of her tab. Her dress hugged her curves, showed off her legs. The black accentuated her pale skin, her blond hair. He touched her arm, the contact necessary, and it calmed him instantly. Most of him, at least. It seemed to have the opposite effect on his erection, but that was no surprise. It wasn't possible to be around her and not be aroused.

"Let's go," she said, as she gathered her coat and purse.

He took her hand and led her to the elevator and they rode up to the suite in companionable silence. It was his turn tonight, and he knew exactly what he wanted to do. He wasn't sure she'd willingly go along with it, but he was going to persuade her.

The elevator stopped twice before they got to the fifteenth floor, and then they were in the hall, at the door, and he pulled the card key out of his wallet.

Once inside, he locked up, then stopped her with a

hand on her arm. She turned, surprised, and he spun her around until her back was against the door, her coat hit the carpet, as did her purse, and he leaned in for a bruising kiss.

His heart pounded as he thrust his tongue into the warm wetness of her mouth, and when she responded with a moan and teasing of her own, he was a goner.

Grabbing both her hands in his, he pulled her arms up over her head, held her captive as he pulled her lower lip into his mouth and nibbled on the tender flesh. Wanting to kiss her everywhere at once, to taste everything, all of her, he settled for the soft hollow at the base of her neck. Her perfume made him ache as he nipped and licked and kissed her, and finally, as he sucked in her pale skin, marking her. It was a childish impulse, but he couldn't stop himself. When she moved her head back baring her neck further, he released her, only to move his lips to her pulse point. The beat of her heart matched his own rapid pace, as if they had one heart instead of two.

"I want you," he whispered against her hot flesh. "Dammit, Susan, I can't get enough of you."

She pulled her hands out of his grasp and he stepped back. "I know. It's so…"

"It's everything," he said, the desire in her gaze stoking the fire inside him. "I don't care who you are. If you don't want to tell me another thing, I'll still be happy. But I want to share myself with you. I don't want any secrets."

He regretted his words the second she turned away. Damn. What was it with him? Was he really this stupid?

"David."

"Yes?" He prayed her next sentence wasn't goodbye.

"It's technically still my turn, you know. Going to the emergency room was nowhere on my fantasy list."

He exhaled, letting the tension ease between his shoulders. "That's not fair."

"I'm not the one who did the half gainer."

"So, you want to try it again?"

She shook her head. "Not yet." She stroked his forehead where the bump had been. "Let's wait till the bruises fade, shall we?"

He grinned as he stepped back then went for his shirt buttons. "It's a deal."

"Hold it."

He raised his brow. She grabbed his hand and pulled him over to the couch. He sat, and then she moved to the other side of the couch and sat.

"Susan?"

"Yes?"

"What are we doing?"

She smiled. "We're talking. Or we will be soon."

"Oh?"

"About you."

Interesting diversion. But it was a step closer to her revealing herself, if he could be honest with her. "What do you want to know?"

"Who was the first girl you fell in love with?"

"Natalie Benson."

"That didn't take long to figure out."

"She was the first. The first is important."

"And where did you meet Ms. Benson?"

"In PS 204. Fifth grade. She sat in front of me for a whole year. She had long, dark hair that smelled like green apples."

"Goodness. Did she return your affection?"

He smiled, remembering. "For a brief, shining moment."

"Go on."

"I followed her around like a puppy, and she tolerated me. Mostly, I think, so she could use my bike. But after weeks of unrequited lust, I finally got the nerve to kiss her. She seemed surprised, but she didn't slap me or scream or anything. I decided to take that as a declaration of love."

Susan chuckled. Her smile grew open, easy.

"But, as in all great tragedies, Natalie left me soon after. Brad Geckler stole her away with the promise of a skateboard. She never looked back, and I never quite got over her."

"Do you know what became of her?"

He nodded. "She moved to Ohio, got married, had kids. Last I heard she was teaching kindergarten."

"Who was next?"

"Next?"

"Your next love."

"Ah. That's tougher. We're getting into the middle school years, and that was just one crushing blow after another. It wasn't until high school that I had any success with the ladies. I think it had something to do with fact that I grew five inches taller in one memorable summer."

"Who stands out?"

"Marie Clymer."

"Tell me."

"She had the softest voice. I always had to lean forward to hear her. It was just above a whisper, and the sound made me crazy."

"Is that all you liked about her?"

"Yes. It was enough."

"What did she say with that magical voice?"

"She could have read the phone book. I still would have been her slave."

"And yet, she didn't become Mrs. David."

"No. She went off to Stanford when I went to Harvard."

"Did you have your way with her?"

He grinned. "She was my first."

"And?"

"I confess, it was over in about two seconds, but that was just the first time. I got better."

"I'll say."

"Are we going to go through my whole sex life?"

"Maybe."

"Are you going to continue to sit all the way over there?"

"Again, maybe."

"Hmm."

"What?"

"This is your fantasy? Listening to me talk about ex-girlfriends?"

The liveliness that had been in her expression died, and he wanted to shoot himself for opening his big mouth. Twice he'd done this tonight. Where the hell was all his training?

She turned, her gaze falling on the window. "My first time was when I was eighteen. He was twenty-five. I was so tired of being a virgin. I met him at a dance. He was a bartender. He took me out to the golf course and we kissed for a long time. That was the good part."

David leaned forward, put his elbows on his knees. He wished she would look at him.

"It was over quickly. He wasn't very...skilled. Of course, I didn't know that. I just wondered why there was so much fuss, you know?"

He nodded, and he wondered if she was looking at his reflection. He couldn't tell from this angle.

"After, he called me. A lot. I told him I couldn't go out with him, that my parents wouldn't let me. He didn't care for that. Shortly thereafter, I went to London to visit my aunt. My cousin Betty told me that he'd gone to my father, told him what had happened. Threatened to tell everyone at the club. Ruin my reputation. My father paid him off. I never did find out where he went. I just never saw him again."

David searched for something comforting to say. Nothing came to him. So he went to her. Cupped her cheek, lifted her gaze to his. Then he kissed her. He couldn't change her memories. He could only give her new ones.

Her fingers slipped behind his neck. The pressure grew, both against his lips and on his flesh. He felt her sorrow, her disappointment, and then it turned into something more.

She stood, wrapped her arms around him hard, desperate. He tried to pull back but she would have none of it. She thrust her tongue in his mouth, pushed her body against his, and God help him, he pushed back.

Her hands went down his back, rubbing, kneading, then to his belt buckle. She unzipped him before he could stop her, and then when she touched his aching erection he didn't want to stop her.

She turned them around, pushed him down on the chair. Got on her knees.

"Susan, wait."

She shook her head.

"This isn't about us."

"It is now."

"Please. Can't we talk?"

She took him in her hand, gripping his shaft firmly, scrambling his thoughts. "Enough talk. No more talk. Just fantasy."

He groaned, cursing himself for the weak fool he was. When she swirled her tongue, even that thought fled. All that existed was the two of them, this moment, her heat. The pressure built too quickly, and then he was past the point of no return. She squeezed him, milked him, made him cry out as he came in a torrent so potent he saw flashes of lightning behind his eyes.

By the time he could breathe again, her head was cradled on his thigh, and she'd tucked him back into his pants as if nothing at all had happened.

For the first time since he'd met Susan, he felt uncomfortable. Not that he didn't appreciate what she'd done for him. But he knew it had been a diversionary tactic.

All he could hope was that the door had been

opened. Sure, she'd slammed it shut, but if she could confess one thing, perhaps she could confess more.

For now, though, he would give her the freedom to hide behind the sex. He only hoped he was doing it out of care for her, and not because he was a selfish bastard.

She confused the hell out of him. But she was worth it.

14

SUSAN KNEW he wanted more. More touching, more talking, more closeness. But she couldn't. She hadn't meant to talk about that long-ago night. It wasn't fair to herself or to David to bring up her screwed-up love life.

She'd had the right idea all along. Stick to sex. Fantasy. Keep reality outside the hotel.

He'd been quiet as she gathered her things. Hadn't complained at ending things so early. But she could tell he wanted to ask her more. Bless him, he held back. She wasn't sure if he'd pressed, she wouldn't have given in, and that would have ruined everything.

They walked slowly to the elevator, his shoulder just brushing hers. The contact felt good. Easy. He pressed the call button, then touched her hand.

A moment later, he turned on her so quickly she cried out in surprise, and then she was up against the wall, her hands in his, pressed tightly above her head.

"I've tried to be calm," he said, through clenched teeth. "I've tried to be considerate and caring and all that bullshit. But I can't leave like this. Not like this. Not because it's sex, but because it's you. Do you hear me? Because I can't get enough of you."

An intoxicating rush of fierce triumph, blinding relief, and pure, unadulterated desire surged through her, sweeping away any vestige of rational thought. She released her hold on reality willingly, surrendering herself to sensation.

David shuddered as he pressed his mouth against hers, forcing it open with a swift thrust of the tongue and claiming it aggressively. As he pushed his hips against her body, showing her his amazing recuperative powers, she shifted until her thigh went between his legs so she could, in turn, show her appreciation. David thrust against her thigh once, twice, then he bent until his lips brushed the shell of her ear. "If memory serves," he whispered, his hot breath making her shiver, "only one of us came so far."

She closed her eyes as he pulled her earlobe into his mouth and nibbled on her like an hors d'oeuvre. "What do you suggest?"

He swiped his tongue briefly around her ear, making her gasp. "I'm going to make you come until you beg for mercy."

"Oh, my."

"And then I'm going to do it again."

She inhaled sharply. "Okay."

He chuckled. "No arguments?"

She shook her head, ready to strip down right there in the hallway, and damn the tourists.

He stepped back, keeping hold of her left hand, pressed the call button, then pulled her into his arms. Another soul-searing kiss made her wish the elevator would never arrive, but it did, and his hand went to the small of her back as he escorted her inside. They were alone, at least for the moment. He stood quietly, although she could feel the thrum of excitement radiate from his body.

"Where are we going?" she asked.

He smiled, a wicked grin that made her weak in the knees, then he pressed the stop button, and the elevator came to a jarring halt.

"What?"

He turned to her, his gaze feral and his nostrils flaring dangerously. "Take off your panties."

"What?"

"Just take them off."

She blinked, knowing she should argue about this. Or at the very least pretend to be shocked. Instead, she hiked up her dress, caught her thumbs on her panties and pulled them down until they dropped to the floor. Her dress fell into place, which made David frown.

"Pull it back up."

Forcing herself to breathe, she obeyed, lifting her dress above the tops of her stockings, above the last vestige of modesty.

"You're beautiful," he said, his voice so gruff, so filled with desire she nearly melted. God, she felt incredibly naked. And so hot.

He moved forward slowly, his gaze traveling from her sex up her body until he found her eyes. She couldn't see a trace of hazel, his pupils were so dilated. And she didn't see his hand slip between her legs. She jumped when he touched her. Stroked the lips of her sex with controlled fingers.

He kissed her then, forcing her back against the wall of the cab, thrusting, sparring with her tongue, his fingers fighting for her concentration against the heavy competition of his kiss.

As quickly as he'd started, he stopped, pulled back, and dropped to his knees.

She arched and moaned when he mimicked his kiss, thrusting his tongue between the folds of her sex. It was unbelievably intense, knowing where they were, that they could be caught. Staying upright was becoming a problem, and then there was nothing else but his tongue and her pleasure and she grabbed his hair and tried not to scream, but it was no good. He never let up, not for a second, and she was already so primed that everything happened too fast. Her muscles tightened, the world shrunk to a very small space, and then she went over the edge, her cry echoing against the elevator walls. As if triggered by her release, the alarm went off, buzzing horribly, signaling God knows who that they had hijacked the cab. David fell backwards, landing on his butt, his eyes still glazed with lust. She dropped her skirt, and tried to look as if she hadn't just been ravished by the sexiest man on earth.

He leaned over, pressed the stop button once more, and lurched to his feet as the elevator went down. He pulled a handkerchief from his pocket and gently wiped his lips, then put the white linen back. He smiled at her. She smiled at him. Then they reached the ground floor, and the doors hissed open.

Susan almost lost it when she saw the crowd waiting for them. The general manager was there, along with a couple of bellmen, several guests and someone from security. David took her hand with a firm squeeze and led her into the lobby. He paused by the manager, and shook his head. "You'll need to have that looked at."

"Of course, sir. I'm sorry."

"It's all right. These things happen."

Susan didn't laugh. She wanted to, oh Lord, she wanted to, but she used her early training and forced herself to smile with just a hint of superiority. David, bless his twisted little heart, didn't even walk fast across the lobby. His back straight, his bearing controlled and elegant—now this was a man to be with in an emergency.

They got to the door, and David pushed it open. As she passed him, she stopped, thunderstruck. Her hands went to her bottom and her face heated with the mother of all blushes.

"David."

Realization dawned on his face slowly. He nodded, letting her know he understood, then ushered her out to the chilly Manhattan night. As soon as the door closed behind him, he burst into laughter.

She didn't see the humor in the situation. "Sure," she said. "Laugh. Those aren't your panties in the elevator."

He did. Laughed until she thought he might be sick. Eventually, she relented, and while the humiliation took the edge off the hilarity, she did have to admit it was funny. Sort of.

When he finally gathered his wits about him enough to function, he pulled her into his arms. His hand slid down her backside. "I love it when you go commando."

"Women don't go commando. That's a male term for a male activity."

"So what do you call it?"

"Naked."

"I like that better."

She wiggled a bit, liking the feel of her dress on her skin a bit more than was wise. "You do realize our coats are upstairs."

He nodded.

"My purse, too."

Again, he nodded.

"We have to go back in."

This time, he shook his head. "No, we don't."

"But—"

"Not yet."

"So we're going to stand out here and freeze so we don't get embarrassed?"

"No. We're going to walk down to the bar on the corner. We're going to sit in a dark booth as far away from other humans as possible."

"And do what?"

His eyes widened in feigned innocence. "Have a drink."

"That's all?"

"Maybe not."

"I see."

"No. But you will." With that, he kissed her, hard, just once, then took her hand and headed for the end of the street.

SHE HAD a mandarin cosmopolitan. He had a dry martini. The booth was in the corner, away from the buzz of the bar where too many single women in stilettos searched for Mr. Right. Or Mr. Right Now. A cell phone rang and half the females in the place lifted their purses to their ears. Susan laughed, and David slipped his arm over her shoulder.

She laid her head against his, a quiet, comfortable, easy silence between them. A contentment he'd never known made him want to stay just like this forever. Okay, not forever. For awhile. And then he wanted to take her back to the suite and make love to her.

The games had been fun, he wasn't about to deny that, but the more he learned about Susan the more he wanted to know. And, truth be told, he was nearly crazy with needing to be inside her.

Her warm palm touched his thigh. "Penny for your thoughts."

"Is it still only a penny? I would have figured ten bucks by now."

She gently squeezed his leg. "You're cute. Did you know you're cute?"

"Cute? Cute is for puppies."

"I love puppies."

"So if I wag my tail—"

"I'll give you a treat."

He smiled. "Woof."

"Come on. Tell me what you were thinking about."

"You."

"Oh."

"And me."

"Go on."

He turned his head so his lips were very close to her ear. "I want you," he whispered.

"You've already got me."

"You know what I mean."

"David—"

"Wait. Don't shut me down yet. Hear me out."

She nodded and a lock of her hair brushed his temple. He closed his eyes for a few seconds, enjoying the sensation.

"Even though I look like a manly man," he began. "Macho through and through, I have one pretty big weakness."

"Which would be?"

"You."

"Oh, my."

"Precisely."

She shifted on the seat until she could look at him. His arm fell from her shoulders, so he took her hand in his.

"I can't stop thinking about you. I know, I've said that before, but the situation isn't improving. It's getting worse. I had no idea I wouldn't be satisfied with the original plan, but—"

She jerked back as if he'd slapped her. "You want to end it?"

"God, no. That would kill me."

"But—"

He lifted her hand to his lips for a kiss. "If all you ever wanted to do from now on was sit in the room and play Parcheesi, I'd be there. It wouldn't be my ideal scenario, but it would beat the hell out of not seeing you at all."

She touched his cheek with her other hand. "So sweet."

"No. Not sweet. Selfish. Terribly, terribly selfish. I want more, Susan. I'm willing to settle for less, but dammit, I want it all."

"All?"

He nodded. "And I'm not just talking about making love. I want to know your name. Where you grew up. What you eat for breakfast. I want to know your friends, and hear your troubles, and I want to read the *Sunday Times* in bed with you."

Susan's hand fell to her lap. Her gaze lowered, too. He should stop now, before he ruined everything. But not saying it didn't make it any less real.

"I would like to see where this relationship can go. It might fall apart, sure, but it might not. You're an incredible woman, Susan, and I like so much about you. But I'm at a handicap here. In so many ways, we're strangers. I'm sorry if this upsets you, but I have to be honest about what I want."

She sighed, stared at her fingers. "Things will change," she said, so softly he almost missed it.

"Yes. Things will change. But things will change anyway. That's the nature of the beast."

"I don't want it to. I want what we have. I want to know you'll be there every Wednesday. I want to play and to laugh and to make love—"

"But we haven't."

"That's just a technicality."

"No, it isn't. Sex is playing. Making love is intimate. Vulnerable."

"That's right. It's vulnerable. And the whole point of this was to leave that crap outside the door."

"What crap? Intimacy? Truth?"

Susan polished off her drink, then played with the rim of the glass as she stared at the cherry, run aground. "People say they don't care about things. But they do. They care, and it changes the dynamics, and then it all falls apart."

David felt at a loss. Her confession was incomplete, and he knew he could coax her into revealing more, but should he? Was it right to bring his training into this? Would a friend, someone who expected nothing, respect her wishes and let it go? Or would a friend try to understand all of her?

"Expectations can be hell," he said, still unsure of his next move. "But sometimes, life can surprise you. Things can turn out better than you ever dreamed."

She frowned, and the slight downward tilt of her lips made her achingly beautiful. "Why risk throwing out something you know works for something you're not sure about?"

"I guess the only answer to that is being very clear about what you want. Short- and long-term."

She looked up at him, her gaze almost accusatory. "You said yourself that it might fall apart."

"You're worth the risk."

She didn't say anything for a long while, but she did study him, her gaze unhurried as she searched his face. "I don't know if I can survive another blow."

He closed his eyes for a moment, and when he looked back at her he saw her fear. She'd clearly been hurt before. Deeply. For all her bluster and eccentricity, he also saw how fragile she was. For Susan, love was all or nothing. He couldn't promise her unending happiness. There was no such thing. But he also couldn't push her into a relationship before she was ready. "All right." He smiled. "I'll just say one last thing, and we won't speak of this again. If you want to climb out on that scary limb, I'll be right next to you. I'll do my best to make sure neither of us falls."

Susan closed her eyes for a long moment, then rested her head on his shoulder. He leaned a bit until his head and hers touched. That was all. That was enough.

15

JANE SPOTTED LEE as soon as she walked into Café Nicosia. She'd never been to the trendy spot on Wall Street, but had heard the food was excellent. Which was good, because she was starving. She shouldn't be—she'd had an enormous breakfast. But with her these days it was either feast or famine. Today was definitely feast.

She walked around the perimeter of the room, knowing if she tried to negotiate between the tables, her stomach would collide with something it shouldn't. As she got closer to Lee, she studied the woman sitting with her, Katy, her friend since college. She was a pretty woman, dark hair in a shaggy cut that was sophisticated and smart. She couldn't tell about her wardrobe, but her makeup was perfect. Jane figured both women were about five years older than her.

"Jane." Lee stood up, a noble thing considering her belly. They tried to hug, but it was too ludicrous, sort of like the dancing hippos in *Fantasia*. Then Katy stood up, and Jane's eyes widened. She was more pregnant than either of them! "What?"

Katy nodded. "I'm due in two weeks."

"Wow, this is incredible. We're all going to have

babies, and they're all going to be friends, and they'll grow up and talk about their mothers as if we're the lamest creatures on two feet. How cool is that?''

Lee laughed. ''Very cool. Now, let's all sit down before we start making the busboys nervous.''

The three of them maneuvered themselves into their chairs, and busied themselves with menus, ordering, polite chitchat, until finally, when they each had their meals in front of them and the glasses had all been filled with their assorted beverages, Lee cleared her throat. ''So, Jane. What's the story with your friend?''

Jane sighed. ''It's not going well. And I don't understand it. I hate to say it, but I think there might be a woman in his life already...''

''But?'' Lee asked.

''Well, I don't want to let this go. David is the sweetest man in the world, but he can be a little vulnerable when it comes to a certain kind of woman.''

''Oh?'' Katy nibbled on her Cajun chicken breast. ''What kind of woman?''

''Let's just say David needs someone sweet. Who won't manipulate him too much.''

''Uh, that would be a puppy,'' Lee quipped.

Jane laughed. ''You know what I mean. Someone with a good heart. Who won't be after him for his money.''

Lee and Katy both laughed at that, and Jane waited for an explanation.

''Susan's loaded,'' Katy said. ''She's like a Rockefeller or something. And in the love department, it hasn't done her any good. Her ex-husband was a conniving bastard who took her for everything he could. Then when she finally risked dating again, the men, and I mean every one, hit her up. She's so discouraged. She doesn't think she'll ever find a man who'll love her for her.''

Jane shook her head, ate some pasta, drank some water. ''I'm sorry, I know she's your friend and all, but I have to ask. Is she bitter?''

''She can be sarcastic,'' Lee said. ''But that's just a defense mechanism. She's scared to death, poor thing. She wants so badly to love someone who will love her in return.''

''Of course she does. Everyone does.''

''She has so much to offer…'' Lee stopped talking and smiled brilliantly. Jane followed her gaze. Across the restaurant, a very handsome man had a matching smile as he headed their way.

''Trevor,'' Katy said. ''Lee's husband.''

''I figured.''

''He's a wine critic.''

''Oh, Charley would love him. He's into wine. Seriously. He's always telling me about fruity bouquets and subtle smoke. I just nod and smile and think about the next episode of *Sex and the City*.''

Trevor arrived at the table and gave Lee a smooch that spoke volumes about the state of their marriage, then he kissed Katy on the cheek. ''Almost there,'' he said, patting her stomach.

''Almost.''

He turned to Jane. ''Trevor Templeton.''

''Jane Warren. Nice to meet you.''

"I don't want to intrude. I just remembered you would be here—"

"Sit down," Katy said. "We're talking about Susan."

Trevor frowned as he took the seat across from his wife. "Susan's a big girl. She can take care of herself."

"You've seen how she's been acting lately," Lee said. "Tell me you're not worried about her."

"Okay. I am. But you've got that Lucy and Ethel look about you, and that can't be good."

"Please." Katy rolled her eyes.

"It's called meddling, Katy, and most people don't care for it."

"Do you really think you and Lee would be together if we hadn't meddled?"

"Yes," he said adamantly. Then he cleared his throat. "Most likely."

Katy pointed her fork at him. "No. You'd still be pretending you didn't love each other, and you'd be dating all the wrong people, and you wouldn't have Junior coming to join you. There's nothing wrong with meddling, as long as it's done with purity of heart."

Trevor coughed. "Purity of heart? Jeez, Katy. What book is that from?"

"It's not from a book. It's how I feel."

"You know," Jane said, "I have to agree with you. If it wasn't for David, Charley and I wouldn't be together." She turned to Trevor. "Charles Warren. My husband."

"Tell us," Lee said.

After another sip of water, Jane leaned back, trying to find a more comfortable position, which was fruitless, of course. "I worked for Charley, and I was madly in love with him, but he didn't even know I existed. He thought my name was Joan. Then, and I know you won't believe this, but I swear it's the truth, I got hit on the head by a plaster cupid."

"What?" Katy nearly choked and had to grab her iced tea.

"I know. But it happened. I had partial amnesia, which sort of manifested itself in making me think I was Charley's fiancée."

Lee looked at Katy. Katy looked at Trevor. Trevor called the waiter over for a scotch.

"David was the one who decided to play it out. He convinced Charley that he needed to let me stay at his place. That he couldn't risk sending me into some deep psychosis or something. And, well, things led to things, and we got married with David as our best man, and now all I want to do is help him find the kind of happiness Charley and I have."

"I think they sound perfect for each other," Lee said. "But Susan's been so, I don't know, weird lately. She hasn't called much. Hasn't met us for lunch. She's even missed our Sunday brunch, which she never does."

"Oh, I love going to Sunday brunch," Jane said.

"You'll have to join us sometime…okay, okay." Lee shook her head at Trevor. "He doesn't have much time. He wants us to keep the conversation on track."

"Such a guy," Katy said.

"Damn straight," Trevor said. "And proud of it."

Lee grinned, blew him a kiss, then turned back to Jane. "Personally, I don't believe in coincidences. I think we were meant to meet at the OB/GYN, and that we're supposed to help Susan and David get together."

"Yes," Jane said. "Exactly."

Trevor shook his head, but he didn't say anything.

"More than that," Katy said. "We need to make sure Susan's okay. That she's not in trouble. I don't like the way she's been avoiding us."

"So, what shall we do?"

Lee put down her fork as if it were a gavel. "We're going to get to the bottom of this, and we're going to make sure Susan and David meet. And we're going to do it before the three of us go into labor."

Trevor sighed as Lee, Katy and Jane toasted their cause.

DAVID STUDIED THE NOTES he'd finished, trying to read the words as clinically as possible. Gordon was due in a few minutes, and he had the feeling it was going to be a tough session. The actor had been front page news in tabloids all over the world with innuendo and accusations about his sexuality. One paper claimed to have a video proving that Jack was gay, and another claimed to have phone tapes. David knew neither was true. Gordon was straight. Not even bisexual. But the tabloids didn't need anything as ephemeral as the truth to build their stories.

So why was David reading the notes he'd made on Susan, when Jack needed his attention? Not that he wouldn't put aside all other thoughts when the man arrived. Thankfully, his obsession with Susan hadn't wormed its way into his therapy. Today, however, was a bit tricky.

She'd said he could have whatever he wanted. He'd interpreted that to mean that if he asked to make love to her tonight, she'd say yes. But would she say yes just to appease him? Did he care?

Yeah. He cared. More than he should.

Maybe Susan was right. That the whole reason he was this entranced was because of the mystery. If he knew all about her, things would change. What he honestly didn't know was if they'd change for the better or not.

He'd had drinks with Charley last night, and that was another reason for doubting himself. Charley was so damn happy. Of course, with a woman like Jane, who wouldn't be? And David envied him. He didn't want to steal Jane or anything, although a clone would be terrific. He wanted the mixture of passion and playfulness the two of them had. He wanted to feel the safety of a rock-solid relationship. Something told him he might be able to find that with Susan. On the other hand…

He kept remembering what Jane had told him. That he always managed to find the fatal flaw in any woman with potential. So far, Susan had given him seduction, fantasy, mind-blowing orgasms, no strings, no neurotic games. No flaws there. But if she filled in the blanks? Was he looking for the details of her life so he could have ammunition?

His buzzer made him start. He closed his file, then pushed the intercom. "Yes, Phyllis?"

"Mr. Gordon is here."

"Give me a minute, please. Then send him in." He clicked off and took a moment to stretch his neck and get out his notebook and tape recorder for the session. He put Susan in his pocket, where she'd stay quite nicely until the business at hand was concluded.

SHE'D ARRIVED at the suite almost an hour early. First, she'd gone to the bar and given a note to the bartender who promised to see to it that David got it when he arrived. Which should be in about ten minutes.

It was his night, and she wanted to make it wonderful for him, even though she knew it wasn't going to be easy for her. He'd want to make love. No stories. No blindfolds. No barriers. Just the two of them in the bed, in each other's arms.

He'd want answers, too.

Part of her wanted it so badly she could hardly breathe. But the fear kept pushing at her, kept speaking to her in low, urgent tones to get the hell out of here while she still had her illusions intact.

She didn't want to lose David. In theory, he should be fine with who she was, with her money, her upbringing. He had money of his own, so what was she worried about?

Sighing, she straightened the pillow behind her back and pulled the sheet up higher on her chest. It felt a bit weird lying there naked, but this was his night, and she knew he'd like it if he found her powdered, perfumed, and his for the taking.

Her mind, not content to focus on the immediate future, went back to her dilemma. There was money and then there was *money*. No one outside of that rare circle understood. The walls were erected for very good reasons. So many were so desperate, would go to any lengths to get a piece of a pie that didn't belong to them.

She could explain about the charitable donations her family made, the trusts, the scholarships, the medical facilities and all the rest until she was blue in the face. It didn't matter. Everyone wanted. All the time. And they got so insulted, so furious when they realized their problems weren't going to be fixed by the Carrington largess.

Thank goodness for her real friends. Lee, Katy, Ben, Trevor, Peter…none of them had ever let the money part get in the way. In fact, they'd been her saving grace. They loved her for who she was. Even when she was bitchy, or spoiled, or depressed. So why wasn't it possible to find someone like her friends? Who's to say David couldn't be another Trevor or Ben?

At the thought, her chest constricted. She'd hoped so many times. Been burned so many times. Love and money didn't seem to mix well. She thought again of the people she knew who traveled in her parents' circle. Were any of them happy? Most had interbred, like pedigreed puppies. But some had gone outside the fold and married the odd doctor or model. She couldn't think of one of those unions that were still intact.

Maybe she would be the one to break the mold. Maybe the stars were in the right position and the gods had smiled down upon her, sending her the perfect man.

Or maybe she just had to accept the fact that if she wanted a relationship, she'd have to pay the price.

The click of the door lock set her heart racing as she let the sheet fall to her waist and fluffed her hair.

Footsteps in the other room. Then quiet. He must be taking off his coat. Was tonight going to be a suit or jeans? He looked incredible in both, but she hoped for the jeans. Nothing was sexier than undoing the buttons on a worn pair of Levis.

"Oh, my... You are the most stunning creature I've ever seen."

She smiled at him in the doorway. "Good answer."

He shook his head as he approached, walking slowly, cautiously, as if he was afraid he'd spook her. It was another one of the things she liked about him.

He'd worn his jeans. Yes. And a gray long-sleeved shirt that fit just snugly enough for her to truly appreciate his chest. Her gaze traveled over the man from his leather boots up his long, lean legs, to the button fly. She blushed at how happy he was to see her. Good old Levis. Those buttons were made to last.

"I can't believe this," he said. "Every time I see you, there's something that surprises me. Something that throws me off guard."

"Is that good or bad?"

"Excellent."

"Phew."

He stopped several inches from the bed. "I could look at you forever."

"I won't always look like this, you know."

He shrugged. "You will to me."

She moaned as she shifted a bit on the bed. That sentence was going to keep her up nights. Fill her dreams. Make her crazy...

"I want to make love with you," he said, his voice so gruff with desire it made her whimper. "But you still have time to say no. To renegotiate."

Her gaze shot down to his fly, then back up to his eyes. "That was very noble."

"You're telling me."

"Don't worry. I'm not going anywhere."

"Thank God," he said as he crossed the short distance between them. He sat on the bed and he touched a lock of her hair. "I don't know what to do first."

"I have a suggestion."

"Hmm?"

"Since one of us is quite overdressed..." She grinned.

"Oh. Yeah. But I'm not convinced that's what I should do *first*."

"Intriguing. What are the other options?"

"I want to kiss you. For a day or two, at least."

"Uh-huh."

"Oh, did I mention that was just your mouth?"

"Uh-uh."

"Yeah. Because I also want to taste every bit of

you. Spend hours and hours memorizing you with my lips.''

''Oh.''

''That's not all.''

He'd done it to her again. Not five minutes alone with him and she was completely, wantonly turned on. Her nipples grew hard and tight. That tingly constriction in her stomach got into the action, and her sex followed the biological imperative and became more than ready to welcome him home. ''Go on.''

''Oh. Yeah. I want to make you come. Over and over again.''

''Selfless.''

He shook his head. ''Do you honestly believe I could watch you and not come, whether I was touching you or not? Hell, whether I was touching myself or not?''

''Really?''

''Really.''

''So what's it going to be?''

He leaned down over her, met her gaze from scant inches away. ''I can't decide,'' he whispered. ''How about I do all three?''

16

DAVID CUPPED HER CHEEK in the palm of his hand as he tasted her. She sighed, and her sweetness went inside him, made him whole again. How was that possible? He hadn't even known he was incomplete until...

Slipping his tongue between her teeth, he explored leisurely; textures, tastes, heat, moisture, everything felt new and sharp. He rubbed her cheek with the pad of his thumb, amazed as always at her softness. Knowing she was naked, knowing he could touch her anywhere and she'd welcome him, intoxicated him. He felt dizzy at the possibilities.

She moaned, and the sound shot straight down to his erection. And when her hand touched the back of his neck, fingers splayed in his hair, light pressure holding him steady, he grew harder still.

Her other hand went to the hem of his shirt, but he stopped her. "Not yet," he whispered, his lips brushing against hers.

"But—"

"It's my night, remember?"

As she nodded, he found himself caught by her gaze. Her pupils were so dilated, he could see his reflection in them. Her long, dark lashes came down for a few seconds, and he noticed the spiky shadows under her eyes.

It was as if he'd finally found the right lens to see through. The rest of the world sat in some vague haze. Yet when he studied Susan's hair, he noticed each strand, the fluctuation of color, the pattern of the strands as they spread over her shoulders.

Her fingers behind his neck pulled him back down, and he chuckled at her impatience. "Anxious, are we?"

"I am. I'm not sure about you, though."

He licked her lips, not stopping until he'd made a complete circle. Then he did it again. Halfway through the second time, her lips parted and he drank in her breath, her scent.

As much as he wanted to stay right where he was for the rest of his life, his compulsion to taste the rest of her was just as strong. He solved the dilemma by kissing the little indentation beneath her moist, pink mouth. Her chin was next. Licking, sucking, nipping…he didn't move until he knew every centimeter. And then he dipped below, to her throat.

Her scent was stronger here. He knew what it was, now. He'd been in Macy's and had gone to the perfume counter. It had taken him a long time to find it, but he had. Boucheron. He'd never heard of it, but now it was a part of him. A sense-memory that would evoke Susan for the rest of his life. Actually, it had been a bit embarrassing—he'd gotten hard the moment he'd identified the perfume.

He kissed her throat just below her left ear, and the intimacy, the eroticism of feeling her blood pulse beneath him made him moan. Her fingers flexed in his hair, massaging his scalp, and he wondered if anyone had ever died from pleasure.

The only fly in the ointment was the constriction in his pants; the pressure would have to be relieved soon. But not yet. Not when he was learning her in a whole new way.

He licked up her neck, then teased his tongue around the shell of her ear. Rewarded with a soft shudder, he moved inside the delicate curves reading her reactions by her fingers, by her tremors. School was in session, and he was determined to be an expert on giving her pleasure.

"David," she whispered.

"Hmm."

"Oh, God."

"What?"

Her head fell back against the pillow. "Just, oh, God."

He chuckled, and she trembled, and screw it, he had to get the damn pants off before he ruptured something. "Don't move," he whispered. Then he stood and attacked his belt buckle. Only, he didn't get far. Her hands stopped him. When he looked at her, her smile turned sly.

David let her have her way. She pushed him slightly back so she could throw off the sheet and sit at the edge of the bed. Her naked flesh glowed in the diffused light of the wall sconce. So beautiful. So female. He marveled again at the softness of women, of Susan in particular. So different from his own skin. Everything with her was velvety curves and silk, where he was sharp angles and calluses. Which was excellent planning on someone's part.

Her fingers on his belt stopped his thought process. As she slowly pulled the leather through the loop, he concentrated on her face. Her rapt expression made her forehead furrow a bit, and she nibbled on her lower lip in a way that made him jealous. That idea fled as she worked on the top button of his jeans.

She paused before moving to the next button. Paused and leaned over, covered the hard bulge of his erection with her mouth, then exhaled. The hot air through the cloth was almost his undoing. As it was, he had to grab hold of the headboard to keep from falling.

It was her turn to chuckle, which she did as she opened button number two. Again, she paused, and this time, instead of a warm breath, she spread open the small V of his fly, pushed down the edge of his boxers and licked the space she'd uncovered.

"Susan," he said, as soon as he'd remembered how to speak again.

"Yes?"

"Oh, God."

"I know. And it's only starting."

He moaned as she moved on to the third button. After it was freed, she traced the entire length of him with one fingernail. Exquisite torture. Knee-weakening, mind-blowing, life-changing torment.

She undid the fourth and last buttons. Knowing he'd never remember later, he pulled the condom he'd brought out of his pocket and tossed it on the bed. Then she answered his prayers by pulling down his pants and his boxers, clearing the way for his erection to breathe, so to speak. Something had to, as he hadn't exhaled since button three.

His pants dropped, and he felt the moist tip of his penis brush against his belly. This was a world-class erection, a seventeen-year-old's hard-on. The urge to beat his chest and yell like Tarzan was strong, but he held himself in check.

All bets were off, however, when she leaned forward and slowly licked his shaft from the base to the tip. As if that wasn't enough, she moaned as if she'd just tasted chocolate mousse. His heart pounded so hard a coronary was imminent, but he didn't give a damn. Well, it would be better if he died after the main event.

Her lips went around the head of his penis, soft, moist, hot. She held him still for a long moment, and then her tongue flicked over the tip. He gasped, and he felt her smile. Then her tongue flicked again, unerringly finding the sweet spot as if she knew his body as well as she knew her own.

His hand went to her shoulder, as much to steady himself as to feel her skin, to intensify the connection between them. If she didn't stop soon, he was going to come, and he didn't want that to happen, yet. He squeezed his fingers lightly as he pulled back.

She let him go with one last lap from her tongue, then looked up into his eyes.

"Oh, God."

She nodded. "I loved that. Hearing you moan. Feeling you shudder. Tasting you."

He lowered himself to his knees in front of her,

then used gentle pressure to spread her legs. "My turn," he whispered. Putting his hands low on the back of her hips, he pulled her forward on the bed, so she rested on her tailbone. Her sex, still smoothly shaved, glistened with moisture. Bending his head, he kissed the inside of her right thigh, then the left. Moving slowly, fighting the urge to take her like a cave man, he continued to nip and kiss the tender flesh of her thighs, teasing her with warm breaths as he reached the juncture.

She brushed a lock of hair from his forehead. When he looked up at her he realized it wasn't an idle gesture. Her gaze was on him, on herself, on what he was about to do. When she spread her legs even farther apart, it was like an electrical discharge, a lightning bolt of eroticism.

He leaned slowly forward, closed his eyes, breathed deeply. A different perfume, musky, private, enticing. This scent, more than flowers and spices, drew him to her. Made him part her nether lips with gentle fingers and stare with wonder and awe, and even a little fear that he wouldn't please her when her pleasure meant everything.

A moan from above, a slight tremor in the thighs. He smiled, thought about making her wait, but discarded the notion. He leaned in those last few inches and with the flat of his tongue, he licked the length of her sex, savoring the salty, earthy, womanly taste. Then he hardened his tongue and explored her inch by inch, listening for her sighs and whispers, for her shudders and her gasps. Learning where her pleasure peaked and waned, then using the information ruthlessly.

She collapsed on the bed, her arms flung out to her sides as she writhed beneath him. He sucked hard, relaxed, then sucked again. Over and over, and she thrashed, pulled the sheet, keened as if he was killing her, and maybe he was. Her hips bucked under him, and it was all he could do to hang on.

She grabbed onto his hair with both hands, pressing herself against him, and then she got quiet as she tensed. A few seconds later, he felt the spasms start from deep inside her.

It felt as though she came forever. Jerky motions, unintelligible words, her right knee digging into his arm, and there was all that heat. He never let up, not until she whispered, "Stop," and pulled his head back.

He stood. She was a rag doll across the bed, a sheen of sweat making her body almost luminescent. Her chest rose and fell with deep, gasping breaths, and the flush of her orgasm hadn't begun to fade yet from her chest or her face.

Inordinately proud of himself, he ran his arm across his mouth, climbed back on the bed, and straddled her. She opened her eyes grudgingly. "Hey."

She smiled. "Hey."

"How you doing?"

"I'm swell."

"Yeah?"

She nodded. "You need to switch careers."

"Oh?"

"Yeah. You need to do that for a living. Psychiatrists are a dime a dozen, but someone with your gifts... You'd turn them away in droves.''

He chuckled. "I'm not this good with anyone else."

"No?"

"Nope."

"You're just being modest."

"I'm not. Susan, I'm not kidding."

Her smile faded as she heard his earnestness. "Why not?" she whispered. "What's different about me?"

"I don't know. I probably should know, but I don't."

"Is it the arrangement?"

"Maybe. But what I said last week is still true. I want to know you. Now, more than ever. Something is going on between us. You know that, right? You feel it?"

She closed her eyes briefly, then met his gaze. "I do. But it's scary."

"Life is scary. Nothing's safe." He moved up the bed so he could see her face better. "But I won't hurt you."

"You won't mean to."

"No. I won't. But you're right. People get hurt. It's part of it all. I can't change that."

"I just don't think I could survive."

"Of course you could. You're strong. You're resilient. And more importantly, you're whole. You don't need me to make you happy, Susan. You don't need anyone for that. But wouldn't it be something to have someone to share it all with? Like we share this bed? These fantasies?"

"David..."

He kissed her lips gently. "It's all right. I won't insist."

"I need time to think."

"I'm in no hurry."

She smiled. "Thank you."

"You're—"

Her hand on his erection opened his mouth and shut down all higher functions. He moaned as his eyes rolled and when she pumped him, his legs and arms trembled so badly he was afraid he'd fall and crush her.

She must have realized the precariousness of her position, because she let him go and pushed him to his side. He didn't fight her. He couldn't have. All he could do was beg her to pick up where she'd left off.

SUSAN WANTED HIM on his back. He didn't seem to have any objections. Once he was in position, she scooted down to kneel between his legs.

His penis arched over the dark curls, the head almost resting on his belly button. She'd never had a particular thing about male genitals, but even she had to admit, his were stunning. She wondered if she should tell him? *David, I think you have a gorgeous package?* No. Not right now. Maybe someday. But man, on a scale of one to ten, his equipment was an eleven. Tight where he should be, just big enough, thick enough. As perfect as the rest of him. With his long, lean legs. The sparse hair on his well-developed chest. And then, of course, there was his face. His unselfconscious beauty. That delectable lower lip.

She leaned down, adjusted her legs, then ran her tongue along the thick vein on the underside of his penis. He jerked under her tongue, and she loved the feeling of power.

She lingered at his glans, sucking the tip of his penis inside her mouth, and after a quick flick with her tongue, she released him and nibbled her way back down to the root. She didn't stop there. She explored him slowly, the soft, furred skin of his testicles, the heat of his inner thighs. She lifted his knees to give her better access, and then she bent down and stroked his perineum until he begged for mercy.

The careful journey continued as she moved back up, and this time, when she reached the head, she took him in her mouth and with consistent pressure, swallowed him as deeply as she could. She licked and sucked and teased him, listening for his cues, learning what he liked best.

When his legs began to tremble, it was time for the next phase. He wasn't going to last much longer, and tonight, as promised, he would come inside her.

She released him from her mouth, which prompted a disappointed groan, then stood on the bed. He stared up at her quizzically, not sure what her next move would be.

She showed him. Placing her feet flat on either side of his hips, she lowered herself slowly. As soon as she could reach him, she tore open the condom and slipped it on him. Then she fisted his erection, holding him in position as she went lower still. Finally, their bodies met. She rubbed the tip of his penis along the entire length of her sex. He appeared to like that, if his death grip on the sheets was any indication.

Then she held him steady as she lowered herself another inch, bringing him inside her. Using every bit of concentration she owned, she moved down gradually, squeezing her internal muscles as he filled her. Finally, he was in her fully. His formidable girth stretched her in the most wonderful way. She sighed as she adjusted to his size. To his shape.

Then she rose up again, as patiently as she'd gone down, inch by aching inch, stopping just shy of letting him go.

He strained forward, the tension in his neck and his face testimony to his struggle not to take charge. Not to thrust into her until she cried uncle.

She lowered herself again, but before she reached the bottom, David whispered something she couldn't understand. "What?"

His gaze found hers and held her steady. "Please."

It was his night. His call. She squeezed her muscles once more. Then she began the ride of her life.

Her own thighs trembled with the effort, her heart beat furiously in her chest, and his gaze—his gaze changed everything. He filled her completely, and it was like nothing else, like no other time in her life. Not with her ex-husband, not with anyone. It wasn't the body parts, the pheromones, the way they'd waited for this moment. It was the look in his eyes. The depth of his longing. The connection between them.

It was too much, and it made her chest ache, and

she looked away, concentrating on her body. His. She pumped harder, faster, and he growled his pleasure, but then, just as she felt sure he couldn't last another moment, his hands went to her hips and he stopped her.

She looked up, confused. He was so close. For him to stop must have been a superhuman effort. "What's wrong?"

He said nothing as he slipped from inside her. Then he was sitting next to her, with his arm around her shoulder. He kissed her gently on the lips, then maneuvered her onto her back. With a gentleness and purpose that made her heart constrict, he moved on top of her, hips to hips, legs to legs, chest to chest. "Look at me," he said.

She closed her eyes, knowing if she obeyed, she would be lost.

"Susan."

It was no use. She had to look. And when she did, when their gazes locked, she couldn't lie to herself any more. She wanted him. Not for one night a week, but for all her nights and her days. For all her years. She wanted him.

She was in love with David, and there was nothing she could do about it...except surrender.

She opened herself to him, and he slipped inside her. After a long, still moment he began a slow, thick rhythm...in her and *in* her and her legs grasped his hips and his face moved closer and his eyes were filled with desire and strength and something she warned herself not to believe.

And then, he came. Every muscle in his body strained as he cried out her name.

In the long, slow minutes that followed, she caressed his back, his hair. Held him tight to her breast. And she prayed with all her heart that she wasn't making the biggest mistake of her life.

17

EVEN BEFORE Susan opened her eyes, his scent told her everything. That she'd fallen asleep in his arms, that the beat of his heart had been a lullaby, that she'd felt as though she'd become a part of him, and still did. They had spent the entire night together.

She shifted a bit in the bed, careful not to wake him. Once settled, she studied his face. So beautiful, peaceful. The dark sheen of his stubble made him appear older, rougher. But that was mitigated by the soft curve of his lips. The lock of hair on his forehead.

Was he the one?

The thought thrilled her and scared her spitless. Either way, she was in big trouble. If he was the one, the man she'd waited her whole life for, there were still no guarantees. He could turn out to be just like Larry. Just like so many others. Although, something told her that wasn't the case.

But how could she trust her inner voice when it had been wrong so often? Because her heart skipped a beat when she heard his name? Because she melted when he touched her? That was chemistry, nothing more.

And yet...

The thought of never seeing him again was unfathomable. She'd already crossed the line. The concept of sex for sex's sake had been good. Solid. Unfortunately, she'd miscalculated badly on her partner.

She should have gone for one of those dangerous Alpha men. Someone named Spike or Mac. A man with tattoos. Who would have ridden her hard, but left her empty.

Instead, she'd found David. Sensitive. Funny. Bright. Interesting. Dammit, he was everything she'd wanted in a man, and some things she hadn't dared hope for.

So what was her problem? Why didn't she wake him up, right this minute, and tell him everything he wanted to know? Fill in all the details, answer his questions? What was this last barrier about?

Fear. Of course.

She sighed with disappointment. She couldn't be one of those women who got burned by love once, and swore off the male race forever, could she? No. Because it hadn't been just once. It had become a pattern, and although her degree had been in English, she knew enough about psychology to understand her bad judgment wasn't simply bad luck. She was the common denominator. In some way, she had brought these men into her life. The problem was, she didn't understand what it meant. Why she found herself hurt time and time again. There had to be a lesson. Only, she had no idea what it was.

Trust? That was certainly part of it. She didn't trust the men in her life to love her for herself...

She held her breath as a curtain opened before her. She'd completely missed the point. It wasn't about the men. It was about her perception of herself. Without the money, without the connections, without the clothes and the galas and all the rest, who was she? She'd defined herself by what she had. Not who she was. Therefore, the only reason any man could love her was for those things. Not for her.

The realization took her breath. On some level, she'd known this about herself, but never with this clarity. The consequences of her beliefs had formed her life. Her loves. Her world.

So where did David fit in? He didn't know about her "things." He knew her for her sexuality. Her sense of daring. Her imagination. Which was fine, but it, too, wasn't who she was. Caring. Generous. A true friend. Petty. Cutting. Funny. Good and bad... thankfully more positive than negative. But David had no idea about those qualities.

"Hey, what's wrong?"

Her gaze jerked to David. How long had he been awake? She smiled, not just because she felt shy about her thoughts, but because she was so very, very glad to be here with him. "Nothing's wrong. Nothing at all."

He narrowed his gaze for a moment, but then he must have decided not to pursue the matter. He kissed her on the cheek then slipped out of bed. "Be right back. Don't go anywhere."

"Deal," she said, watching him walk toward the bathroom. Damn, but his ass was a fine piece of work. Oh, yeah. His shoulders and legs were, too.

She rolled to her back and stared at the white ceiling. The sun slipped through the slit in the drapes and there was a swash of light cutting the room. Their room.

What did she know about him? That he was a psychiatrist. That he was funny, smart, sexy, handsome, debonair, suave, sophisticated, kind, persistent... All admirable. Okay, all wonderful. But that wasn't David. That was the part of him he showed her on Wednesday nights. The spit-and-polished, courtship version.

Who was he when he was cut off in traffic? When he had the flu? When his team lost the playoffs? And, more importantly, what did he believe about himself? The scary, below the surface belief? He wasn't married. For a man as gorgeous as him to be single at his age meant something was going on.

The bathroom door opened and she scooted out of bed to do her thing there. On the way, David stopped her. Pulled her into his arms, her back to his front. His erection, not as grand as last night's, but no small matter, rubbed against her backside. He kissed her shoulder, then rested his chin there. "Hurry back."

"I can't hurry back unless you let me go."

"Then don't hurry back. Stay here."

"Uh, David. This isn't an optional trip."

"Oh." He released his hold. "Sorry."

She turned to him. "How about you order us some coffee? Maybe some muffins or something."

"How long will it take room service to get here?"

"I'm not sure."

"Then let's wait. Unless you're desperate."

"Ah. I see. A man with priorities."

He nodded.

"Hold that thought," she said, then she darted into the bathroom.

David closed his eyes and thought about his dentist. Not that he had a thing for his dentist, who was in his fifties, portly and wore a terrible toupee, but thinking about his dentist was one of the least sexy things he could imagine. He went back to the bed and put some pillows against the headboard. Then he lay down, hands behind his neck, ankles crossed, and waited.

His erection, always formidable in the morning, eased up a bit, thanks to Dr. Green, and so did his sense of urgency.

She'd stayed the night. That should tell him something, right?

He felt different. The night had changed him. Changed them. He wanted to move to the next level, whatever the hell that was. And if she said no? He didn't know what to do about that, either. Better not to jump to conclusions. There would be plenty of time to panic later.

So successful was his decision to relax, that he nodded off until Susan sat down on the bed. He woke with a jerk, to the sound of her laughter.

"So much for hurrying."

He followed her gaze to his now inelegantly flaccid penis. "You do know, of course, this is only temporary. In fact, the wind is picking up as we speak."

"The wind, huh?"

He nodded. "Nautical metaphors. Jibs, sails, mainmasts, all that. Very manly."

"Right. I'm turned on."

"I figured."

She grinned broadly and flopped down beside him. "Hey, David?"

"Hey, what?"

"What's the worst thing about you?"

He leaned forward to look at her face. She didn't appear to be kidding. "The worst thing?"

"Uh-huh."

"I don't know."

"Well, if you did know, what would it be?"

He thought for a moment. Not that he didn't have anything wrong with himself. It was just difficult picking out the worst flaw. "I overanalyze everything."

"Have you overanalyzed us?"

"God, yes."

"What were your conclusions?"

He brushed a loose hair off her cheek. "That I don't know what the hell I'm doing."

Her laughter made his body stir. That hadn't happened to him before. Orgasm by laughter? He'd have to take her to comedy clubs often.

"Me, neither," she said.

"What's yours?"

"I don't believe in myself."

"You? Come on. You're incredibly confident. That's not something you can fake."

"I'll give you that. Put me in a social situation and I hit the ground running. But in a one-to-one relationship? I don't do so well."

"Why not?"

She looked up at him but he had the feeling she

wasn't really seeing him. Finally, she said, "You know what? I want to talk about this. I do. But not now. I still have too much to think about."

"Okay. If you're sure."

"I'm sure."

"Fair enough. But may I ask something before we jump on each other?"

"Sure."

"What's your last name?"

Susan's smile faded. The openness that had been there seconds ago changed into wariness. She opened her mouth. Twice. But the name didn't come.

DAVID READ THE ARTICLE for the second time, absolutely appalled that something so untrue could be in print. It was the topper in a week that had been one nightmare after another. He wasn't sure of his footing with Susan. Not even sure she would come to the hotel tonight. Things had been awkward between them Thursday morning, and he hadn't been smart enough or quick enough to make them right. He'd snapped at Phyllis, been sharp with Jane, lost his cool with a cab driver and now, he was being maligned as a money-grubbing celebrity sycophant, at best, in a magazine that boasted over eight million readers.

The bastard reporters had followed him. Taken pictures. Manipulated images. Plastered his face on the cover, no less, in a pose with Jack just provocative enough to make people wonder about their relationship. They'd done enough research about his client list to make outrageous assumptions, and spurious assertions.

David knew it had more to do with Gordon than with him, but still. It was libelous, and all lies, and he wanted to do something about it. Right now. Preferably, find the son of a bitch who wrote this and smash his face in.

He tossed the rag on his desk, and turned to face the city. The article didn't really matter. It was an annoyance, but one that shouldn't damage his career or reputation. If he was going to have celebrities as clients, then this was one of the hazards. He'd get over it.

He wasn't so sure about getting over Susan. Not that she'd said it was over. In fact, she hadn't said much at all. After he'd asked her last name, she'd done everything in her power to get out of the room except trip the fire alarm.

The hardest part to face hadn't been her unwillingness to reveal her name, but that clearly the night of making love hadn't meant much more to her than a satisfying orgasm—or five. But that was beside the point. The earth had moved for him, and not for her. He wanted more than she was willing to give. Which meant he had some choices to make. Did he want to continue with the game, as planned? Or would it be too difficult to have this lopsided relationship? The irony of the situation wasn't lost on him. He'd always been the one to pull back, to withhold. Now, he was on the other side of the fence, and he didn't care for it one bit.

Dammit. He loved her. He could, if he tried, convince himself that he didn't. That it was infatuation. That he'd fallen for the mystery and not the woman.

But that wasn't the case. He knew what he needed to know about her. Her last name, her secrets, they were details, that's all.

Falling in love with her wasn't the smartest thing he'd ever done. But perhaps it was the most honest. And potentially the most painful. So what next? How was he supposed to convince her that she should take a chance on him?

He had no idea. All he knew for sure was that he'd be at the hotel tonight.

SHE'D GONE TO PICK UP the new issue of *The New Yorker*. But as she reached for the magazine, her gaze caught on a familiar face. No. Couldn't be. Why would David be on the cover of a tabloid? She lifted the paper off the stack. It *was* David. David and Jack Gordon, standing together. Very close to each other. The picture was grainy, clearly a candid shot. Taken without their knowledge, she felt sure.

She flipped open the magazine and found the article that went along with the art. By the time she finished reading it, she felt sick.

According to this, David catered to a very elite crowd, actively seeking out the rich and famous to enhance his reputation. Although it didn't spell out his relationship with the movie star, the subtext was that the two of them were more than doctor and patient.

Of course she knew the tabloids couldn't be taken at face value. The reporters had no qualms about telling lies and planting false information. But in her experience with this particular paper, there was always some truth to the allegations.

Her friend Denny had been caught with that rock singer, what's-her-name, and while neither of them left their spouses, or got involved in wild orgies, the basis of the article had been accurate. Denny did have an affair with the singer. And then there was that piece about Alex and Kim, and that had turned out to be mostly true.

Was any of this true about David? Maybe not. Probably not. But if it was...

No. She couldn't believe there was even a grain of truth to this garbage. David wasn't the type to solicit famous clients. He'd never stoop to anything that low.

He certainly wouldn't pursue her just because she was rich and connected. No. He didn't even know her last name, for heaven's sake. It was ridiculous.

She put the paper down, and hurried away from the newsstand. Paranoia. That's all. It was her fear talking, not the facts.

LEE DUCKED into a doorway and signaled Katy and Peter to stay back. This cloak-and-dagger stuff was really taking it out of her, and she leaned back for some deep breaths. No wonder there were so few eight-months-pregnant private eyes. And Katy had it worse than her.

But they'd managed to follow Susan all the way to the upper West Side, and now it appeared they'd hit pay dirt. Susan had gone into the Versailles hotel.

Katy and Peter reached her doorway, and although

it was tight, given the expanse of bellies, they all squeezed in.

"So, it's a hotel," Katy said.

"Probably meeting someone," Peter added.

Lee nodded. "Probably a married someone."

"Oh, man," Katy said, leaning against the brick wall. "Maybe we shouldn't go any further. I mean, if she is seeing a married guy, what are we going to do about it? She's over twenty-one. She can make her own decisions."

"But," Lee asked, "if she is involved with something unsavory, don't we owe it to her to help? We're her friends."

"I don't know." Peter peeked around the edge of the doorway, then ducked back. "I'd just feel better knowing she was safe. I don't care what she's doing as long as it's not dangerous."

"So come on." Lee led and the other two followed past fashionable boutiques and restaurants. Once they got to the hotel, Peter went inside on a reconnaissance mission, while Katy rubbed her aching back and Lee commiserated.

It wasn't even five minutes later that Peter stuck his head out the door and waved the women in.

Lee hadn't been to the hotel before, although she'd read about it. The décor made her think of movies from the forties, men in fedoras, women with big shoulder pads. It was the kind of place Barbara Stanwyck would have met Richard Widmark for a steamy assignation.

"She's back there," Peter whispered, nodding toward the bar.

"Is she alone?" Katy asked.

He nodded. "Come on." He took them up to the door to the bar, then pointed to the hallway that led to the restaurant. "You guys hang out there. She won't see you if she walks out."

"What are you going to do?" Lee asked.

"I'm gonna see what I can see." Peter grinned. "I've always wanted to be James Bond."

Katy shook her head. "I've always wanted to be Tinkerbell. It ain't gonna happen."

"Spoilsport." Peter waved them away. "I'll do my skulking in private, thank you."

Lee followed Katy to their post. Katy leaned against the wall while Lee peeked around the corner, watching Peter.

He checked the bar, then ducked back, flattening himself against the door. A moment or two went by, and he dared another look. This time, the coast must have been clear because he hightailed it to the other side of the door. Looking more like Inspector Clouseau than James Bond, Peter jumped when an elderly couple passed him by. He smiled like an idiot, then looked at her with panic-widened eyes.

She signaled him to come over, but he shook his head. He got into position by the door, then leaned over so he could see inside.

That's when Lee saw the man approach. He was tall, lean, dark-haired and good-looking. His gaze fell on Peter and he stopped still. His expression grew cold as he stared, and Lee got a sick feeling in her stomach. She waved at Peter, but he wasn't looking her way. She cleared her throat, loudly, but that didn't work either. The man took a step toward Peter, and when Lee saw his hands curl into fists, she gave up all pretense and ran, as much as she could, to avert disaster.

The stranger was quicker, and before she could say a word, he had Peter by his collar, and was hauling him away from the door.

"You son of a bitch," the man said, his voice putting the fear of God into Lee. "You've gone too far this time."

"Hey," she said, grabbing him by the sleeve. "What are you doing? Let him go."

"I've had it with you damn reporters."

"Reporters?" Lee tugged harder on his sleeve. "Hey, stop it. We're not reporters."

Peter held his hands up above his head, as if he was in the middle of a bank robbery. "I'm an actor. Don't hit my face."

Just then, Katy came huffing up beside Lee. "Let him alone," she snapped.

The man looked at Katy, then at her stomach. His expression changed from murderous to confused as hell. When he caught site of Lee's belly, he let go of Peter, and backed up a few steps. "What the..."

"We're—" Lee's voice froze as Peter moved away from the man and bumped right into Susan.

"Peter?" she said. "What?"

"Uh-oh," Katy whispered.

Peter grinned. "Hi."

But Susan wasn't looking at her friends. Her gaze was on the man who'd almost pummeled Peter. The way she stared at him made Lee cringe. There was a world of hurt in her eyes, a mask of betrayal.

"You bastard," Susan whispered as she walked past the man.

He reached out to grab her, but he wasn't quick enough. "Wait. Susan. Hold on."

She shook her head, walking as fast as her high heels could carry her, straight through the lobby and out the door.

The man looked stricken. He gave the three of them one last puzzled yet furious glance, then he lit out to follow Susan.

When he'd gone, Peter slumped against the door. "We screwed up," he said.

Lee looked at him with withering sarcasm. "You think?"

18

SUSAN STOOD in the street, her arm extended to hail a cab, tears blurring her vision. He *did* know her name. More than that. He knew her friends. He knew it all, and he'd never breathed a word. How could she have been so stupid?

"Susan."

She whirled around at the sound of his voice. "Don't," she said, then she turned around searching desperately for a taxi.

"Susan, wait. You don't understand."

She ignored him, and when he touched her arm she jerked free. "What's to understand? You lied."

"Lied about what? I don't have a clue what's going on—"

"No? How do you know Lee, then, huh? How do you know Peter and Katy?"

"I don't. I've never seen them before in my life. I thought they were reporters."

"Oh, please. Don't insult my intelligence."

"If you think about it for one minute you'll see that—"

"That I trusted you?" She swiped her eyes with the back of her hand, furious that she was crying.

His face changed, and her stomach dipped crazily,

because the look he gave her wasn't good. Not good at all. So disappointed. Incredibly sad. "You didn't," he said. "You didn't trust me at all."

"But I—"

"You didn't even trust me with your name."

He stared at her as if he didn't know her, and she wanted to turn the clock back, to make the last fifteen minutes disappear. No. She'd have to take it all back. From that first night on, because he was right. She hadn't trusted him. Or herself. "David—"

He shook his head. "It's no good, Susan. I can't do this. I can't be with someone who doesn't trust me. Who can't be open."

"I want to be."

"Look, I don't know what your secret is. And up till about five minutes ago, I didn't give a damn. I would have still loved you if you turned out to be a bank robber. But that's not the issue, is it? It all comes down to trust. Without that, there's nothing." He stepped back, shook his head, and walked away.

He was right. She'd shortchanged them both. And it had cost her...everything.

"David," she called out.

He stopped, but he didn't turn.

"My name is Carrington. Susan Carrington."

Seconds ticked by as she prayed for him to come back to her. Her prayer was answered. God said no.

DAVID SIPPED HIS SCOTCH as he stared out the window of his apartment. His view wasn't spectacular. A few stores across the way, an apartment building much like his own, a reasonably busy intersection. It didn't matter, though. He wasn't really seeing much of anything. Except her.

Susan Carrington. The name had been familiar, but he wasn't able to place it. When he'd reached home, he'd done a search on the Internet. Then he'd understood. At least, he understood her reticence. She was an extraordinarily wealthy woman. Most people wouldn't think of that as a problem, but he knew better. Not from his own experience. He was well-off, but miles away from her league. He knew from his clients. Who'd learned quickly not to trust. Who surrounded themselves with family, or childhood friends because the people they met now were only interested in the persona. The lustrous star.

It was lonely, and scary, and she had every reason to be gun-shy. To a point.

After all the weeks, all the intimacy they'd shared, she didn't know him. Not at all. And what did he expect? They were bed buddies, nothing more. His mistake was coming to care for her.

The phone made him jump, and he debated picking it up. He didn't want to talk. But it could be his service. He sighed as he lifted the phone. "Hello."

"David. We need to talk."

"Not now, Jane, okay?"

"Yes, now."

"Jane. I'm not in the mood."

"Too bad. Because we're coming in."

He heard the key in his lock, and cursed his foolishness for giving Charley his spare. Jane walked in, her cell phone still in her hand. Charley followed, then closed the door.

"What are you drinking?" Jane asked.

"Scotch."

She wrinkled her nose. "You have milk?"

He nodded.

Jane turned to Charley, squeezed his hand in some private, husband/wife signal, then she headed for the kitchen.

Charley came over to the couch, perpendicular to the chair David had occupied for the last several hours.

"What's going on?" David asked. "You usually don't break and enter. Especially not when I'm home."

"Technically, we didn't—hell, that's not the point."

"What is?"

"You've been seeing someone."

He nodded.

"Susan Carrington."

David stared at his scotch. He must have had a lot more than he'd thought. "How do you know?"

"Jane."

"She's a psychic now?"

"No. She's a buttinsky."

"That much I knew. How does it pertain to me?"

"She met this woman at the obstetrician's office. They got to talking. Jane told her about you, the other woman had a friend...they wanted to fix you up."

"Okay," he said, still not getting it.

"The woman she met was Susan's friend."

"The pregnant one!"

Charley nodded. "Hence the obstetrician."

"But wait, you mean they met accidentally, and all this was a coincidence?"

Charley nodded again. "Turns out Jane found out about the doctor from her personal trainer, who specializes in pregnant women, which is how Lee found out about the doctor."

"Same trainer."

"Yep. They figured it out tonight."

"I see."

"And when Jane heard about what happened at the hotel, she insisted we come over."

"Of course."

"So, uh, what did happen?"

"I was a jerk."

"Oh."

David took another sip of scotch. Charley stared at him. The silence was comfortable, if short-lived.

Jane came in, holding her glass of milk. "So, talk," she said.

"About?"

"Susan. What's the deal? Have you been seeing her for a long time? Why didn't you tell us about her?"

"The deal is, I didn't even know her last name until today. It was supposed to have been private."

Jane sat down next to Charley. "Go on."

"There's not that much to say. We got together. On Wednesday nights."

Jane's brows rose. "To, uh—"

He nodded.

"Cool."

David smiled. "It didn't work out quite as we'd expected."

"Why not?"

Dammit. He didn't want to discuss this. He certainly didn't want to tell Jane the ugly details. But it was Jane. And she'd know if he was lying, and she wouldn't let up until he'd spilled it all. No use delaying the inevitable. "It was supposed to have been sex with no strings. Strings developed."

She put her glass down. "What kind of strings?"

"Nothing much. Just that I fell in love with her. Which is crazy, because I don't even know her."

"It's not crazy," Jane said softly. "Charley fell in love with me when I thought I was someone else."

"That was crazy, too."

"But look how great it turned out."

He did. He stared at the couple sitting so close together on his couch. Charley's arm was over her shoulder. Her hand was on his thigh. They belonged together. "I'm not Charley," he said. "My luck isn't that good."

"I've never met Susan," Jane said, "but I have met her friends. And they're good people, David. Top drawer. They love her, and they only have good things to say about her. In fact, before we even knew, we decided you guys would hit it off."

"Pardon?"

"You know what I mean. This was kismet. Fate. I mean, how else do you explain it? It's sort of like a cupid falling on your head, don't you think?"

"Jane, honey. The woman didn't trust me enough to tell me her full name."

"So? Trust takes time."

"Trust takes a leap of faith."

"Okay. Then take that leap. Trust your instincts. Find her. Tell her you love her."

"She doesn't want that."

"Yes, she does. I promise."

"How do you know? You said yourself you never met her."

Jane tried to lean forward. It didn't work. Her stomach got in the way. So she relaxed against her husband instead. "I know you. I know how long you've been looking for the right woman. How you dated so many women, and never found what you were after. David, has it occurred to you that maybe not knowing everything about Susan gave you time to get to know her? To love her? That if she'd told you everything up front, you probably would have found some reason to leave her, too?"

He closed his eyes. "Yeah, it has occurred to me."

"And that maybe, just maybe, you're grabbing on to whatever you can as an excuse to escape?"

"Yeah, that has occurred to me, too."

"So? What are you going to do about it?"

He opened his eyes. Watched the red light on the corner turn to green. "I don't know, Jane. I wish I did."

SUSAN SNIFFED, then wiped her eyes, grateful she hadn't put on any mascara before her friends had come over. It would have been all over her face if she had.

"Was it that you thought we wouldn't approve?" Lee asked.

Susan shook her head. "No. It wasn't anything like that. It was just...private, that's all. It wasn't ever supposed to be anything but, you know, sex."

Lee looked at Trevor. "Yeah, we do."

Susan sighed. "You'd think I would have learned by watching you two, huh?"

Trevor smiled. "Hey, if it's any consolation, we were just as stupid for a really long time."

"Thanks, Trevor, that makes me feel a hundred percent better."

He grinned weakly, then leaned back on the couch.

"Okay," Peter said from his perch on the ottoman, "so what's done is done. The question is, what now?"

"What do you mean, what now?" Susan blinked back fresh tears. "He's gone. It's over. I blew it."

"Susan," Katy said, "don't be a jerk. It's not over until I say it is."

Susan laughed, even though she didn't want to. "Guys, I know what happened."

"Tell us," Katy said.

"I did."

"In detail."

She sighed. Drank some orange juice. Crossed her legs in the big chair. "He said I didn't trust him. That I never trusted him. That there couldn't be a relationship when there was no trust."

"And?"

Susan looked at Ben. "And what?"

"There has to be more."

Susan closed her eyes, remembering with terrible clarity what David had said. The hurt on his face. The hard line of his mouth just before he walked away. "He said he didn't know what my secret was, and until I'd been such an ass, he didn't give a damn. He said he still would have loved me if I'd been a bank robber…"

Susan stopped talking. Somewhere, in her peripheral vision, she saw Lee look at Katy. Peter look at Ben. Trevor look at Lee.

"Uh, Susan?" Lee said. "Did you just say what I think you said?"

She nodded slowly.

Peter stood. "Well, that changes everything, then, doesn't it?"

This time, Susan shook her head. "Does it? He still walked away, Peter. I just didn't realize how much I was losing until it was too late."

HIS LAST PATIENT had left an hour ago, but David still sat in his office chair, playing with paper clips. Thinking about her.

Was she on her way to the hotel? Would she be disappointed when he didn't show?

It was better this way. Come on, it was sex. That's all. He'd romanticized the situation. Made it much more than what it was.

So why the hell did he feel like this? Like he'd lost something vital?

Dammit. He was supposed to be a smart man. People paid him to help with their problems. And he didn't have one clue what to do.

If he went…what would be different? Sure, he knew her name, but he also knew the kind of baggage that came along with being a Carrington. Would she ever believe he didn't love her for her money?

Did he love her? Could he get past her fortune, or would it change him, as she feared?

He wanted to believe it wouldn't, but he couldn't be absolutely sure. That's what trust is for. Faith. Whatever happened, if the relationship was solid, they could work it out. At least, in theory.

He closed his eyes, disgusted with himself for over-analyzing everything again. He'd been second-guessing himself all week. What did he know of love, anyway? Nothing. Except that it felt like home when he was with her. That she made him want to slay dragons. That he wanted to spend the rest of his life getting to know her.

But he also wanted her to lean on him. To need him. To trust him. And he needed to trust her right back.

His cell phone rang. "Dr. Levinson."

"David, it's me."

He sat up straighter at the urgent tone of Charley's voice. "What's wrong?"

"Jane is going into labor. Can you come to the hospital?"

"I'm there. Give me twenty minutes." He hung up and grabbed his coat. He knew the hospital, knew the obstetrician, knew the procedure. Jane was a healthy young woman, and even though the baby would be early, there was no reason to think anything would go wrong.

But his heart was in his throat as he pressed the elevator button over and over again. Jane was in labor. With his godchild.

He wished he could share this with Susan.

THE PHONE WOULDN'T LET UP, and Susan had to make a decision. Get out of the tub and answer the damn thing, or drown herself. It wouldn't have been so bad if she hadn't had the mud mask on, but wasn't that just her luck?

She opted to get out of the tub, although the way she was feeling it might have been more merciful to go for drowning. Wrapping a towel around her as she headed for the bedroom, she tried to think who would call her like this.

David.

No. He hadn't called all week. He could have, and he didn't. That pretty much summed things up. Besides, even if he did call, he would have left a message on her machine. She couldn't see him hanging up and dialing again and again.

She grabbed the damn thing off her headboard. "Hello?"

"Thank God," a voice said breathlessly.

"Peter, what is it?"

"Katy's gone into labor."

"What?"

"*Now.* She's in labor, and she wants you there. At First Memorial. Fourth floor maternity. I'll meet you there, okay?"

"Yes, yes. Oh, God." She hung up, tossed her

towel in the corner and grabbed the first clothes she laid her hands on. Katy was in labor. Unbelievable.

Her hands shook as she pulled up her jeans, and she had to take off the sweater and turn it right side up, but then she shoved her feet in some loafers, grabbed her purse and coat and she was out of there.

The hospital was about fifteen minutes away by cab. If she could get a cab. Oh, God. She wished David could have been with her.

IT TOOK HER thirty-four minutes. Breathless, palpitating minutes. The overriding thought was of Katy, of course. Of her health, and the baby's, and Ben and all the promise that lay in front of them like some glorious tapestry. But David was with her, too.

The cab driver, a peculiar man of undetermined heritage, honked his horn and gazed at her strangely in the rearview mirror during the entire journey. She ignored him for the most part, but his brows were so thick that his puzzled looks gave him one big, dark brow, and frankly, it was disconcerting.

When they finally rolled up to the hospital entrance, she threw him some bills, more than she should have, but what the hell. She slammed the door behind her, and rushed into the lobby and straight to the elevators.

Alone until the third floor when a couple of obnoxious teenagers got in and giggled hysterically. Susan wondered if she was going to be the last to arrive. If she'd be able to see Katy. She had no desire to see the actual birth. That gave her the willies, but she would like to be there before and after.

A baby. A human child. They hadn't wanted to know the sex, so just like in the movies, they'd hear the news upon arrival. Susan couldn't help hoping for a girl. It was the dresses, of course. Too cute for words.

When she finally arrived at the fourth floor, she had to make her way down a long hallway, following red painted lines on the floor to the maternity ward.

Breathless and shaking, she turned the final corner. There, on the blue vinyl couches were Peter and his Andy, Lee and Trevor, two Hispanic men she'd never seen before. And David Levinson.

19

"WHAT ARE YOU DOING HERE?"

David looked at her oddly, as if she should have known. Then he cleared his throat. "My friend is having a baby."

"Jane?"

He nodded, still standing three couches away. "Some coincidence, huh?"

"Yeah," she said. "We seem to attract a lot of that."

Peter stood up and waved at her. "Susan? Could I speak to you, please?"

"Can it wait?"

Peter looked at Lee and Trevor, then shrugged. "Sure. Why not."

She was about to say thanks, but then David took a step. And another. And she found herself frozen. She wasn't ready for this. Not even a little. She was still so unsure, not of David, but of herself. Which might not matter a bit if he didn't want her back.

If only she could say the right thing, know the best way to...

David smiled.

And it all fell into place. The confusion disappeared, the doubts lifted, and she knew, without question or pause, that none of it mattered because she loved him. Loved him with all her heart.

She didn't care that it was a wildly improbable coincidence that he was here now. She didn't care about anything except the fact that he was coming to her. That his eyes welcomed her. That his lips had curved into a beautiful smile.

He stopped an arm's length away. "I'm glad you're here."

"Are you?"

He nodded. "I've done some thinking this past week."

"You, too, huh?"

"Yeah. This situation, it's not easy. There are complications."

"Sure," she said, trying to find her bearings. "Yes. I know. Complications." Her voice sounded normal, at least she hoped so. Oh, God. She'd done it again. Misinterpreted the signals. Wanted him to be something he wasn't. Stupid, *stupid*. But she didn't move a muscle, blink an eye. She wouldn't let him see he was breaking her heart. After all, it wasn't his fault. Not really. She was the one who'd botched this up. She'd wanted to keep her distance, to not get involved, and she'd done an admirable job. "It's okay. It was just the, you know, the, uh, situation."

"Susan?"

"Hmm." She blinked, fighting tears. Wanting the earth to swallow her whole.

"All I'm saying is that it's complicated. Not that it's over. At least, on my part. But if you—"

"What?"

"I said, if you—"

She shook her head. "Before that."

"Oh." He grinned. "I said I don't want it to be over."

"You don't?"

He shook his head this time, slowly from side to side, his gaze never wavering.

She couldn't stand it. She dropped her purse and her coat where she stood and rushed into his arms. He pulled her close, hugging her so tightly she could hardly breathe. She didn't care. It wasn't over. She hadn't ruined it.

"Honey?"

"Yes?" She leaned her head on his shoulder, closed her eyes, wallowed in the feel of him against her.

"I figured out a few things."

"Tell me."

"Well, people don't ever really know other people. Not at first. It takes time for that. Years."

She nodded.

"What matters is the connection between two people. The way they approach life. The dreams they share."

"Yes. That's so right."

"And see, what I think...I think you and I, we connect."

"Oh, God, we do."

"And that we share a lot of dreams."

"Uh-huh."

"And I think I want to spend the rest of my life getting to know you."

That was it. The tears spilled over, and she trembled like a leaf as she pulled back to look at him. Even through the blur, she could see he meant what he'd said. That he did want her. Despite her foolishness. Despite her fear. "I want that, too."

"Yeah?"

She nodded. "You fell in love with me, not knowing my name."

"How could I help it?"

She smiled. "I fell in love with you at the scarf counter."

"No. Not that first day?"

"Yep. I didn't admit it to myself. But it happened that fast. That hard."

"Wow."

"David? Why aren't we kissing?"

He grinned shyly, which wasn't like him.

"Is it because of my friends?"

"Not exactly."

"What?"

He ran his index finger down her cheek, then turned his hand so she could see. It was green. Mint green. As in her face mask. She leapt back, covering her face. "Oh, God, I forgot. I ran out so fast. Oh, God."

Her so-called friends laughed riotously as she spun around, searching for the rest room. Once she saw the sign, she ran, and she didn't stop running until she was at the sink.

Green. A bright green face. No wonder. She splashed herself with water, scrubbing until there wasn't a speck of mask left. She'd never been so hu miliated. David must think she was an idiot. What kind of person leaves the house in a mud mask?

She reached blindly for the paper towels, but someone put several in her hand. After she'd dried off, she turned to thank the kind stranger. Only, it wasn't a stranger at all.

"David."

He smiled. "You know, I'd love you even if you were purple."

She sighed with happiness. He *was* the one. Go figure. After all the heartache, after all the angst, she'd found David. And David had found her.

He pulled her into his arms and kissed her. Kissed her like crazy. Kissed her until she melted right into him.

A collective, "Ahhh," made her jerk back. There, standing in the doorway of the maternity ward ladies' room, were her friends. Lee, Trevor, Peter, Andy, Ben and Katy. Another very pregnant woman who must be Jane stood in front of a handsome devil, who must be Charley.

"Wait a minute," she said. "Katy? Aren't you supposed to be having a baby?"

Katy's face reddened. "About that. We couldn't figure out how to get you two together."

"Really?" David nodded at Jane. "I suppose you had no intention of giving birth tonight either?"

She shook her head. "But it worked, didn't it? You two are together. And you love each other. And it's so wonderful."

David squeezed Susan's shoulder. "I suppose so."

"Suppose my ass," Jane said.

Everyone laughed. Except Katy. Whose face wa■ even redder than before. "Uh, guys? Guess what?"

With that, the bathroom cleared as Ben hustled hi■ wife to the nurse's station, followed by the entire en■ tourage. David and Susan were alone. Together.

"Want to get married?" he asked.

She nodded. "Oh, yeah."

His smile faded a bit. "But won't that mean givin■ up Wednesday nights?"

"Not a chance. I'm going to call the hotel tomor■ row, and tell them to reserve the suite for...well, fo■ ever."

"Forever. That has a nice ring to it."

Epilogue

Two Years and Six Months Later...

SUSAN AND DAVID hurried to the large table at the Broadway café where the gang, including Jane, Charley, and three highchairs for the toddlers, waited.

"About time you got here," Peter said.

"We were delayed," David said, as he pulled out the chair for his wife.

Lee shook her head. "You snooze, you lose. We already ordered."

Susan smiled. "That's okay."

"At least we ordered you coffee." Trevor pushed the carafe toward her.

"Thanks, but no thanks."

Lee blinked. "Are you serious? You without coffee? Are you sick?"

"Nope."

"Oh, my God..." Lee stood up, her hands going to her cheeks, like that kid who'd been left home alone.

Susan grinned. David beamed.

Jane squealed and jumped to her feet. "I don't believe it."

Katy got up, too and the women went into a group

hug, forcing the waitress to turn around and go back to the kitchen.

Ben looked at Trevor, who looked at Charley, who checked with Peter and Andy.

"Shall I tell them, or should you?" Peter asked.

"I'll do the honors," David said as he stood, and pulled Susan away from her friends, and into his arms. "Gentlemen, and ladies...we're pregnant."

Applause broke out around the table, as David kissed her again. But the sound of a throat clearing hushed the group, and all eyes went to Katy. "Not to steal your thunder or anything..."

Susan's brows shot up. "Are you kidding?"

"Nope. We were waiting for you guys to get here to make the announcement."

"Uh, guys?"

This time, it was Lee who pulled their attention. "I haven't gotten the official word yet, but the little pink plus sign looked pretty convincing."

As if they were at Wimbledon, everyone turned to look at Jane. "Nope. Not me." She put her hand on her tummy. "At least, I don't think so."

Susan sat down next to David. As the rest of her friends chatted and ate and congratulated each other, her gaze was on her husband.

She thought about their wedding at City Hall. Nothing elaborate. Just the gang. Just love. Just a promise. And in the months that followed, the journey of discovery that had changed everything in her life. David wasn't just the man of her fantasies. He was the man she could lean on. The man she could comfort. The man who shared her secrets.

She wasn't at all sure how things turned out for Scheherazade. Maybe she and the king got married. She hoped so.

All she was sure about was that the fairy tale had come true for her. Not just on Wednesday nights. But every night.

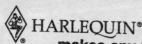

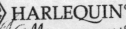

Coming in January 2002 from Silhouette Books...

THE GREAT MONTANA COWBOY AUCTION
by
ANNE McALLISTER

With a neighbor's ranch at stake, Montana-cowboy-turned-Hollywood-heartthrob Sloan Gallagher agreed to take part in the Great Montana Cowboy Auction organized by Polly McMaster. Then, in order to avoid going home with an overly enthusiastic fan, he provided the money so that Polly could buy him and take him home for a weekend of playing house. But Polly had other ideas....

Also in the Code of the West

Available at your favorite retail outlet.

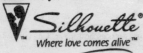
Silhouette®
Where love comes alive™